COLLEGE AND CRIMINALS

THE HEMLOCK INN MYSTERIES BOOK 2

JOSEPHINE SMITH

WESTERN COAST PRESS

*To Max, for keeping me
laughing every day*

1

The Hemlock Inn was quiet that Sunday morning, as if it didn't know what would happen only a short time later. I was in the bistro, like most mornings these days. Hank's fresh-baked blueberry turnover was the perfect treat to get my day started.

"What flavor do we have today?" Tracy Williams, the Hemlock Inn's general manager, approached my table.

"Blueberry," I said, nodding to the turnover on my plate. "Very tasty. You should hurry; a lot of people heard about the new dish, and the bistro's been busy this morning."

The inn had seen an uptick in visitors in the past few weeks. We'd hired extra help on the weekends, from the full-time cleaning crew to additional staff at the front desk. Last month, a dead body and a charity auction had drawn more guests to the inn than was normal for this time of year. October was typically a quieter month before things picked up for the holiday season, or so I'd been told. We'd all had to work extra hours to keep up with the demand.

Business was booming, and I was slowly settling into my new role as owner at the Hemlock Inn. After turning down an offer from a prospective buyer last month, I'd spent a few nights questioning my decision to take on this business. But the buyer had wanted to smooth over all the quirks of the Hemlock Inn that made it special, which would've made my Aunt Sylvia roll over in her grave. Besides, things were looking up for us now, and I was grateful I'd turned down the offer.

"Don't worry," Tracy said, walking past me, her black dreadlocks swinging down her back. "Hank knows to put one of these aside for me each morning." She winked as she passed my table, her nose ring twinkling in her dark-skinned face.

We'd lost the bistro's long-time chef when I'd shown up —the Frenchman hadn't loved the idea of working some-place with so much murder—but Hank, who'd been working as a busboy, had been a wonderful replacement. Everyone who came to the bistro loved his food, and we'd had more diners than ever before. The dead body found onsite last month may have also drawn these people in, hoping for more drama. I, however, was looking forward to a quiet month as we prepped for the busy holiday season.

I smiled, wished Tracy good luck, and turned my attention back to the *Pine Brook Times*, the town's local newspaper. My eyes skimmed over an article about a wild turkey who'd been caught after terrorizing the residents of a Holliston neighborhood for weeks, finally getting relocated to a nearby turkey pasture. The residents of the neighborhood had named the turkey Gerald, and of course he was featured on the front page of this small-town newspaper. I brushed a lock of dark curly hair out of my face as I read.

When I'd shown up in Pine Brook last month after inheriting the Hemlock from my aunt, I didn't think I'd be able to handle it. One violent confrontation with a killer later, and I wasn't quite ready to give up this place. After a cool start, Tracy eventually warmed up to me, and we'd been running it together ever since. I didn't even mind leaving sunny California for dreary Washington state in the fall.

"Reading about Gerald? Miles was so sad to hear they'd relocated him." Estelle Adler, a regular at the bistro, popped into the seat across from me. She gestured to the newspaper when I looked up in question. "I think Miles is going to make a trip out to the turkey pasture to see if he can find Gerald. I told him he was more likely to get bitten by Gerald if he gets too close, but he wouldn't listen to me."

Estelle and her husband Miles had been two of my first friends when I'd shown up in Pine Brook. The seventy-year-old couple had a penchant for danger and had roped me into solving a murder. Now that things had calmed down in town, it appeared they were looking for more danger to keep their lives interesting.

"Tell him I wish him luck." I tapped the picture in the newspaper. "Gerald seems like a nightmare."

"I noticed Nadia tapping at the computer out there," Estelle said, referring to the front desk clerk. "Is she finally figuring out how the security cameras work?"

I let out a groan and hung my head dejectedly. We'd installed security cameras in the front and back of the inn after a dead body had been found in Sylvia's office last month. Rather than keep us all safe, the whole staff had spent the past month struggling to get the cameras to work properly. I'd already wasted several hours last weekend trying to get them to function. They kept replaying the same thirty minutes of filmed footage over and over again, like some kind of deranged, boring rerun on TV.

"I think we need to call the installation team again. They

said the cameras should be working by now, but clearly we're doing something wrong."

"Well, at least things have quieted down since last month," Estelle said, sipping the tea the server, Penny, had dropped off at the table. "I can't imagine we'll have another murder again soon, can you?"

"Knock on wood," I said with a laugh, tapping the table. "I'm surprised, though. I would've thought you'd be itching for another murder to solve."

"Even I can admit when it's good to take a break. Pine Brook can only handle so much death. Any plans for the day?"

I opened my mouth to respond, but shut it quickly as a brown-skinned woman came through the main door of the bistro. She searched the room, a duffle bag in one hand, her curly dark hair pulled up into a bun, a bright green hat clutched in her other hand, and her dark brown eyes the same color as mine. What was my sister doing here?

"There you are!" Chrissy squealed and hurried over, wrapping her arms around me.

I patted her back, uncertain, catching the eye of Estelle, who seemed very surprised by this occurrence.

"Chrissy," I said, finally catching my voice as my sister pulled away from me. "What are you doing here?"

"Well, I'm here to see you, of course," she said, smiling and turning to Estelle. "Oh, I'm so sorry. Am I interrupting your breakfast?"

"Of course not." Estelle smiled and held out her hand. "I'm Estelle Adler. It's a pleasure to meet you."

"Great to meet you, too," Chrissy said, shaking her hand. "I'm Simone's sister."

"Why don't I give you two some space?" Estelle asked, standing as Chrissy took the other seat at the table. "I'm sure you have a lot to catch up on."

"Thanks," Chrissy said with a wave, grabbing the turnover off my plate and popping the last bite into her mouth. "Holy cow, this is good." Her face morphed into a look of ecstasy. "You didn't tell me how good the food was in this place." She set the hat on the table between us and leaned back in her seat.

"Chrissy, what are you doing here?" I repeated. Where were her husband and daughter?

"Like I said, I'm here to see you," she said, grabbing my coffee and taking a sip. "I thought I'd surprise you. Surprised?"

Oh, I was way past surprised.

2

Chrissy rambled on about her trip up here, about how her husband Mark was in the middle of a big trial and working late most nights in the office, and that her daughter Hannah's school was on some kind of fall break, so she'd been staying with Mark's parents in San Diego for the week, and that it seemed like the perfect time to get away.

"Thanksgiving is next month; why would Hannah have a fall break now?" I asked, incredulity creeping into my tone.

"You know these California schools; even for the young kids, they have all kinds of weird traditions and breaks. Last spring, she had six days off for 'mental health.'" Chrissy added air quotes. "I fully support prioritizing our kids' mental health, but those six days off with Hannah home and nothing to do really meant *my* mental health was completely shot."

"But what about your work?" It had to be challenging for a college professor to leave in the middle of the term.

Chrissy waved her hand flippantly. "I haven't taken any time off in years. The department will do fine without me.

Besides, I've wanted to come up here for weeks. You've really got some place around here!" she remarked, looking around the bistro.

I tried to see the dining room through her eyes. It was packed today and more or less running like a well-oiled machine—if you ignored the cobwebs in the corners we couldn't quite reach, and the dishes Hank managed to knock over whenever he came out from the kitchen.

"I still can't believe Aunt Sylvia left you this place," Chrissy said. "I mean, clearly, you're doing something right here, but it doesn't really seem like you. And I can't believe how different it looks from when we were kids."

She was right; there had been a lot of changes over the years. When I'd first shown up, the inn had lost the shine it had when we were kids. Tracy and I had done a lot of work trying to bring it back to that original state. We'd done a good job of it, but there were still a few places that needed sprucing up. Still, we were making progress.

The green hat Chrissy had set on the table was fuzzier than I had initially noticed. I pointed to it. "What is this?"

"Oh, do you like it?" She pulled it down over her head and struck a pose, laughing. "I got cold in the airport and picked this up at one of the shops before leaving security. It's truly heinous, but it's keeping me warm." She stuck the hat into her bag.

"How long are you staying?" I asked, taking a sip of my coffee.

"I was thinking for a week," she said, setting the duffel bag on the floor by our feet. "I had a lovely chat with the girl at the front desk, and she said she could find a room for me. Everyone is really so nice in this place, aren't they?"

I nodded my agreement, trying to forget about the

murderer I'd uncovered last month. Maybe not everyone was all that nice.

"How have you been?" Chrissy asked, finishing off my coffee. "Find any other dead bodies?"

I laughed, not sure if she was kidding. My true-crime-obsessed older sister had been jealous when I'd stumbled onto a dead body last month, and she had wanted all the details after I discovered the killer. I hoped she wasn't trying to get involved in another murder investigation while she was here. I wasn't sure how to break it to her that Pine Brook was a one-murder-a-century kind of place.

I was saved from having to share any of these inner thoughts with my sister by the appearance of Tracy. "How much do you think we'll get for this?" She set a brown vase on the table, her gaze sweeping to my sister. "Oh, I'm sorry if I interrupted."

Chrissy smiled and held out her hand. "I'm Simone's sister," she said, introducing herself.

Tracy shook her hand, her eyebrows raised. "I didn't realize Simone's sister was coming for a visit."

"That's my fault," Chrissy said apologetically. "I surprised her."

"Happy to have you here," Tracy said with a smile.

"Are you selling that?" Chrissy pointed to the brown vase. "It's beautiful."

I had to agree. It was ceramic, lovingly shaped, with flowers etched onto the side.

"There's an antiques fair coming to town," I explained to Chrissy. "Tracy is going through all the inn's items to see if there's anything worth selling."

"I'm not sure if I'll find anything, but I figured I should try," Tracy said with a shrug. "Your aunt was always antique shopping over the years, and she was bound to have picked up something valuable."

Ever since Tracy had mentioned the antiques fair last week, she hadn't stopped inspecting every single item in the inn, in the hopes that she'd score big with something. While my aunt had done a great job of decorating the place, I wasn't holding out too much hope that Tracy would find a seventeenth-century treasure.

"Oh, I should mention, I was thinking we should start looking for a new apartment for you," Tracy said to me.

"What? Why?"

"We'd get a lot of money out of that suite if we can start offering it to guests. Besides, I'm sure you want your own place, right?"

I narrowed my eyes, but nodded in agreement. Why was Tracy trying to kick me out of the inn? Aunt Sylvia had been living onsite up until her death, and they didn't seem to mind not offering the suite to guests then. Did Tracy not want me around so much? Or was I reading too much into her words?

Chrissy glanced at her watch. "I'll let you two get back to work. I should get settled in my room and check my email. Need to make sure none of those college students have gotten too whiny in my absence. We'll catch up later," she said to me, standing and leaving the dining room.

"So, that's your sister," Tracy said slowly, taking a seat. "She seems...nice."

"She is. I'm just shocked to see her here. She didn't call or anything."

I'd planned to invite my sister and parents to come see the inn at some point, but I figured it would be after I'd had a bit more time to settle into my new life, possibly after the holidays. Instead, Chrissy had sprung this visit on me, and I was struggling to reconcile these two parts of my life in my head.

Tracy turned her gaze back to the vase, holding it up close to her face so she could study the detailing along the bottom. I ignored her close inspection of a vase that was probably from T.J. Maxx and took a sip of my tea.

Why was I so anxious about Chrissy's visit? Was it simply surprise at her sudden appearance, or was I anxious because someone who knew me as an irresponsible teenager was here to watch over my new business venture?

With two doctors for parents and an esteemed college professor for a sister, I'd had my share of insecurities as an adult. I'd hoped that by making a name for myself in Pine Brook, I could feel like I was doing well and finally had something that was all mine. Chrissy turning up like this didn't mean that couldn't happen.

"It's going to be okay," Tracy said, cutting into my thoughts. She seemed to realize that I was grappling with something internally. "Chrissy will be here for a few days, and then you can send her packing and not invite her back for six months. That's the rule when it comes to family members visiting." She smiled to soften her words.

"You're right. I think I need a minute to process everything. But I'm sure it'll be fine. I mean, what could possibly go wrong?"

AFTER FINISHING my breakfast and spending some time balancing the inn's various accounts, I got Chrissy's room number from Nadia and headed up the stairs. Chrissy had had enough time to get settled in her room; it was now time for her to answer some questions about why she was here.

The Tudor-style Hemlock Inn had dark wood inside and outside, with lace curtains along the windows and paintings hung from every wall. Tracy made sure we had fresh flowers on every surface, and I'd taken to placing the glass jars full of pebbles from the beach that my aunt collected throughout the inn. Guests always reported that they loved the small details like these.

I knocked on Room 14, where Chrissy was staying. A beat passed, then she opened it in a rush.

"Simone! Didn't realize that was you. Come in, come in," she said, stepping back and waving me into the room.

Room 14 was set up in the same way as all the other rooms on the second level: queen-sized bed pushed up against the far windows; an armoire standing at the far right wall, and a rickety antique desk and chair pushed up against the opposite wall, facing the bed. What set the rooms apart was their design. The rooms had initially been styled with floral patterns when Sylvia first bought the inn: marigolds and roses and peonies and lilies. I could remember how the inn looked when Chrissy and I visited for the first time as kids. I'd thought the wallpaper might peel off the wall and strangle me.

After hiring Tracy, she and Sylvia had tackled the rooms first and redone them completely, focusing instead on an outdoor motif. Each room was stylized like an outdoor destination around the world. Room 14 had coral reefs, seashells, and bottles of sand scattered about the room. The bedspread boasted dolphins jumping out of the ocean, and it rippled whenever you moved it, like they were actually swimming across the fabric. It was still cheesy, but less so. I'd asked Tracy about redesigning the rooms, but she said this new design and motif had become such a staple of the inn, she didn't think people would appreciate changing it up.

I took a seat on the bed, steering clear of the dolphins jumping, and watched my sister. She'd started unpacking, the armoire thrown open as she hung up her clothes. Apparently, she was the kind of person who unpacked all of her clothes as soon as she arrived at a new destination.

"Were the dolphins your idea, or Tracy's?" she asked, nodding to the bedspread.

I smirked. "That's all Sylvia. Why? You don't like them?"

She wrinkled her nose and turned back to the armoire. "I just hope they don't jump off the bed and attack me while I'm sleeping. You know how mischievous dolphins are."

Clearly, she'd been watching too much Animal Planet, but I kept my thoughts to myself.

"Tell me again what brought you up here? I figured you'd plan a visit with Mark and Hannah for the first trip up." My sister loved her plans.

She shrugged, her voice muffled by the armoire door. "Like I said, the timing worked out for a visit. Hannah and Mark were busy with other things, so you're stuck with me. I thought you'd be thrilled to see me."

"I am," I said hurriedly. "It's just unexpected. I'm surprised you didn't call."

"Sorry about that. Everything happened so suddenly. Plus, I thought a surprise might be fun." She popped out of the armoire with a grin. "All right, all done! How about a tour? It's been so long since I've seen the Hemlock Inn, I'd love to see all the changes."

"Sure, let's take a tour," I said, standing and smiling. A tour was easy enough. Plus, I was proud of this place; I wanted to show it off.

Chrissy slung her purse over her shoulder and headed

to the door. I grabbed her arm as she passed, slowing her walk. I couldn't ignore the fact that my responsible older sister had surprised me with a visit, leaving behind her husband and young daughter. Something about this whole situation seemed off.

"Are you sure everything's okay?" I softened my tone. "No issues at home or anything?"

Chrissy smiled and placed her hand over mine. "Of course, everything's fine. Can't a girl come see her successful baby sister?"

She gave my hand a squeeze and walked to the door, while I tried to ignore the fact that her smile hadn't quite reached her eyes.

This was all fine.

We started the tour in the courtyard situated between the lobby and the bistro, which I always wanted to show off. Tracy and Sylvia had remodeled the courtyard the previous summer, and we were still very proud of how it had turned out. Chrissy made the appropriate noises as she walked around the space, *oohing* and *aahing* over the fountain against the back wall. She leaned in close to study the etchings in the fountain.

"Simone, there you are!" Ron Chapman, Sylvia's longtime lawyer, entered the courtyard and headed over in our direction. "I was hoping we could go over the financials for next quarter and make sure we're all aligned on the numbers." He slowed as he saw Chrissy.

"This is my sister," I said, introducing the two of them once he was near us. "Ron's our lawyer, and a close friend."

They shook hands, Ron standing up a bit straighter at "close friends."

"I didn't realize Simone's sister was coming into town," Ron said, looking between the two of us.

"Neither did she," Chrissy said with a laugh. "I thought I'd surprise her."

"Well, these can wait." Ron waved the files he'd been holding in the air. "I'll let you two get back to things. I'll pop on over to Tracy and see how she's doing."

Chrissy and I watched him leave, the gurgling of the fountain in the corner the only sound in the courtyard. After a moment, Lola the beagle trotted into the courtyard and came over to us in search of pats. The three of us continued on the tour.

The rest of the tour was a success, with Chrissy and I reminiscing about our childhood memories at the inn, sprinkled in among all the comments about how much it had changed. By the time we sat down for dinner at the bistro, I was ready to talk about the present.

"How's Hannah doing?" I asked once Penny had taken our dinner orders. Hank had been marinating brisket all week in preparation for the Friday night rush, and I'd encouraged Chrissy to order the special of the night.

Chrissy took a sip of the wine Penny had brought us. "She's fine. She's starting to learn basic fractions in school. I'm terrified about when she gets to the hard stuff in high school. I became a professor in the social sciences for a reason—math gives me hives."

"And Mark? How is he?"

"Fine. Not much to report. I can't wait to eat."

It was like pulling teeth to get anything out of her about her family.

"Chrissy. Please, talk to me. What's going on? Why are you here?"

"Can't I visit my sister? I need some time away from home, that's it. Please, let me have a little break from everything." Her face was sincere, her tone pleading and low.

Fine. If she wanted to spend a few days at my inn and avoid her problems, I wouldn't get in the way. I moved us onto lighter topics, asking how she liked her room. We had more than enough time to get into why she was really here later.

3

The next morning, I was tallying up receipts at the front desk when Chrissy came down the staircase. She was dressed in jeans and a dark sweater, her curls down and framing her face. Dark bags hung under her eyes.

"Everything okay?" I asked once she came over to the front desk. "Did you sleep all right?"

"Actually, better than I have in months." She leaned against the front desk and surveyed the lobby. Was she trying to make it harder for me to study the dark circles under her eyes?

"I've been dealing with insomnia for the past few months," she went on. "Doctor says I'm stressed. These beds are wonderful, but it's going to take more than one good night's sleep to get rid of these bad boys." She waved her hand under her eyes.

I shuffled the last of the receipts back into their folder and stuck the folder into the filing cabinet under the front desk. "Well, I'm finished up here for now, so why don't we get some breakfast? Hank's coffee should help get rid of those things in no time."

Chrissy's smile was grateful, and I led her back to the bistro. It was a busy Monday morning, but I'd told Penny we were going to stop by for breakfast, and she'd reserved a table for us by the window.

"I'll be back with some coffees," Penny said, passing us each a menu as we settled into our seats.

"And whatever pastries Hank is baking," I said, the scent of warm dough hanging in the air.

Penny winked and nodded, leaving to put in the order. I stretched my legs out under the table, pointing my toes forwards and backwards. I'd snuck in a run that morning and could already feel the soreness building in my legs.

Chrissy flipped open her menu, her gaze down. "What's good here?"

"You can't go wrong with any of the specials."

Hank spent the entire week trying out new specials to premier on weekends, when we were at our busiest. I'd had the eggs Benedict a few days ago, and that was at the top of my list to try again.

Penny returned and dropped off two mugs of coffee, a platter of cream and sugar, and two chocolate croissants. I bit into the warm pastry, my eyes automatically scanning the room.

My gaze landed on a small group standing at the entryway to the bistro. It was a group of two men and a woman, and one of the men was tall, over six feet. He was so tall, in fact, that he had to duck his head as he walked through the doorway. I hoped he wasn't here to stay at the inn; he would not fit on our beds.

I turned back to Chrissy. "Ready to order? What looks good?"

She looked up, opening her mouth to answer, then stilled as her eyes widened at something over my shoulder.

I turned to follow her gaze, then gave a start. The tall man had walked up to our table. He had dark skin and dark hair, cut short. A small diamond earring sparkled from his right ear, and he was wearing dark blue jeans and a green hoodie.

"Chrissy. Hi." His voice was deeper than I expected, his eyes on Chrissy.

She gave a tiny squeak, then cleared her throat. "Elijah. What are you doing here?"

I looked back and forth between the two of them, my eyes narrowed. Who was this man? What were the odds of my sister running into someone she knew in Washington? As far as I knew, she hadn't been to the state in years.

"Brunch with a couple buddies," he said, pointing his thumb over his shoulder.

The people he'd walked in with were sitting at a table across the room, staring at us. They waved when they saw us looking.

"I don't mean to interrupt your breakfast, but I saw you from over there and thought I should say hello," this man went on. He smiled down at us, his dark skin creasing at his eyes as he did so. I guessed he was in his late thirties, possibly early forties.

"No interruption at all," Chrissy said, clearing her throat. Her eyes were still wide, her voice monotone.

Silence fell between the two of them, and I coughed. Chrissy jumped.

"Sorry, of course, this is my sister, Simone," she said, gesturing to me.

I smiled up at this man. "Pleasure to meet you." We shook hands, his large hand absorbing mine into his.

"Elijah Norris," he said. "Like I said, I didn't mean to interrupt, but I had to say hello."

"Elijah is a professor," Chrissy explained. Her voice held no emotion. "We met during graduate school on the East Coast, though we haven't talked in a few years."

"Wow." I raised my eyebrows, unable to keep the skepticism out of my voice. "How fortuitous for you to run into each other at my inn."

"I've heard great things about the brunch." Elijah's grin was infectious. "I live in Holliston, but I wanted to try it out."

I smiled, pleased that Hank's reputation was spreading outside of Pine Brook.

"Chrissy, how long are you in town for?" Elijah asked her. "We should catch up while you're here. I'm a professor at the college in Holliston," he explained to me. "Sociology department."

Ah. The same department as my sister.

"I-I'm not sure if I'll have time," Chrissy stammered. "I'm sure you're so busy, too."

"Not at all. I can make time for you," Elijah said, and Chrissy gulped.

She pushed back from the table and stood, the sudden movement causing our cups to rattle on the table. She nearly tripped over her chair backing away from the table.

"I, I actually need to get something from my room," she said. "It was nice seeing you." She spun on her heel and hightailed it out of the bistro, almost knocking over a couple people in her path.

Elijah and I stared after her in silence. What was that all about?

"Great meeting you," he said, giving another tiny smile and backing away from my table.

"Enjoy your breakfast," I said as he walked back to

where his friends were sitting, my gaze still on the door to the bistro.

What was wrong with Chrissy? Why did she dash out of here like that? It was like she'd seen a ghost, or something. Who was this man, and why had he scared away my sister?

I stood, motioning to Penny that we were finished at the table. We clearly weren't going to have breakfast anymore, and I needed to get answers out of Chrissy. She'd been acting odd since she showed up, and I deserved an explanation.

My knock on her door went unanswered. I pressed my ear against the door, but I couldn't hear anything on the other side. Where was she?

"Looking for your sister?" Nadia had come up the stairs behind me, gripping a plastic bucket and a mop. "There was a spill by the ice machine," she explained when I stared at her items.

"Yes, I am looking for Chrissy. Have you seen her?"

"She bolted down the stairs a couple minutes ago. Left the inn entirely. I thought you two were having breakfast?"

So did I. Why did she leave so suddenly?

"Thanks," I said to Nadia, my mind already miles away. I made my way back to the lobby, my thoughts spinning.

What had caused Chrissy to flee like that? Who was that man in the bistro? Why had his presence scared her away?

Once downstairs, I poked my head into the bistro. That man, Elijah, wasn't sitting at his table with his friends. I snagged Penny as she passed by with a tray of drinks.

I gestured over to the table with my chin. "Do you know where the third guest at that table went? He knows my sister, and I wanted to check in on how their breakfast was going." The lie came out easily.

Penny's eyes flicked over to the table, but she shook her

head. "He left a couple minutes ago. I saw him heading out of the bistro while I was wiping up another table. Maybe he went into the lobby to get something?"

The lobby was empty when I first came downstairs, and, after poking my head back in, I confirmed it was still empty, save for one inn guest reading a book in front of the fire-place, but that wasn't Elijah.

Drat. Where was he? And where was Chrissy? Had the two of them gone off together somewhere? Or was I reading more into this situation than I needed to? Yes, Chrissy was evasive about her reasons for being here, but that didn't mean she was running off with practical strangers. Still, it wasn't like her to run away like this. Something must've spooked her.

I slipped my phone out of my pocket—a call should clear things up with her—but a message came through as I did.

Gone to town to get Hannah a souvenir. Let's meet up later tonight. xo Chrissy

At least she was texting. I replied that I had inn business to take care of all day, but could make some time for her at dinner, then slipped my phone into my pocket. If she wanted to spend the day like a tourist, I wasn't going to stop her. I had work to do today anyway. I'd let her cool off, then confront her later tonight about what was going on. She wasn't going to get away with this evasive act anymore.

4

The rest of the day passed quickly. I spent the time folding freshly washed linens for guests, unclogging the toilet in Room 7 because the next guest was checking in early and the cleaners wouldn't be around in time, and on the phone with Pamela, our coffee vendor, who was trying to charge us more for the same services.

"I don't care what your other customers are paying. We have a contract, and you can't change it with no notice like this. I expect we'll see our next shipment tomorrow on time, like always. Is that understood?"

"Fine, Simone," Pamela said with a sigh. "You can't blame me for trying, right?"

I could, in fact, blame her for trying to squeeze more money out of us, but I held my tongue and said goodbye. When I'd first come to the inn, I hadn't realized how many vendors would try to cut corners with us.

"Sylvia, you were much better at this bargaining than I am," I muttered as I made a note in my ledger to indicate the coffee order had been dealt with.

I'd always known my Aunt Sylvia to be a kind woman

with a penchant for roses and tea, but she'd had to be a ball-buster to get anything done around here. I was more and more impressed with her every day.

"Simone, glad I caught you." Nick Yoshida, our produce vendor, stood at the front entrance to the inn. He was no longer wearing his typical torn jeans and ragged flannel, but instead had changed into creased pants, a button-down shirt, tie, and blazer. The cut of his blazer accented his physique, the whole look coming together to give him a red carpet-ready look. He could really wear a blazer well. He strode over to the front desk, a leather binder in hand.

"You look nice," I blurted out, unable to hold back the compliment. My cheeks flushed, though fortunately my dark brown skin hid the pink.

Nick did look nice, and we should all give each other more compliments. That's what I told myself, at least, to hide my embarrassment. Why did seeing this guy sometimes turn me into a school girl with a crush? These flutters in my stomach could not be good for me.

Nick blushed, bowing his head bashfully. "Ah, man, I hate this gorilla suit. I'd give anything to be in jeans all day, but running a business comes with some responsibilities, as I'm sure you know." He held out the leather folder then, motioning for me to take it. "I'm actually heading to the bank to discuss a loan for the farm, and I need to get the signatures of all of my clients. I would've sent an email, but Pine Brook National Bank is old-fashioned and likes the wet signatures."

Understanding dawned as I took the folder and flipped to the page indicated. Ever since his father had fallen ill a few years ago, Nick had taken over running his family farm. While the farm was successful, and Nick had a knack for produce, he'd expressed his disdain for all the business-related work he had to do as a result. If that work got him in blazers and Italian shoes on a regular basis, I wasn't complaining.

"How's your dad doing?" I signed my name on the line indicated on the folder, scanning the sheet. The page was a summary of all the produce Nick had delivered to the inn over the past year, totaling up to a number that caused my eyebrows to rise. We sure did get a lot of food from him.

Nick shrugged, taking the folder back and slipping it under his arm. "Some days are good, some are not so good. Winter is always tough for him; it was the hardest time of the year when I was growing up because the colder weather made it more challenging to grow consistently, and he was always stressed about our ability to make it through the season. And, now that he can't help out as much as he used to, I know it stresses him out to not know exactly how things are going with the farm. I keep him updated as best I can, but it's not the same."

I nodded, my heart breaking at the thought of his father feeling useless at the farm he put so much time and energy into over the years. Nick's grandfather had come from Japan in the '40s and built the farm from scratch, then Nick had taken responsibility for the farm when his dad got sick a few years ago. Still, I knew he didn't enjoy all the responsibility, either. It seemed like both men would prefer it if things went back to the way they were before. Life wasn't like that, though. We had to learn to live with what we had, even if we never wanted it in the first place.

"Well, thanks for this," Nick said, tapping the folder and glancing down at the time on his phone. "I need to get going if I'm going to make my appointment. I'll let you get back to business," he added, nodding to the ledger spread in front of me. He chuckled, very aware of how much I hated tallying these numbers, then waved and left the building.

Thoughts of Nick's farm and his father and the sacrifices he was making for those he loved flashed through my head. For all the ways our families manage to push our buttons and make things challenging, we would still do whatever we could to help them. I knew that firsthand.

I finished my work around six o'clock and headed up to Chrissy's room to see if she wanted to grab dinner. She'd had an entire day to come up with an explanation for why she was here; now it was time to hear it.

However, there was no answer to my knock. Had she not come back to the inn? I'd been so focused at the front desk and working back in the office, I hadn't noticed if she'd returned. I'd just assumed she'd be here for dinner. I pulled out my phone and gave her a call.

The phone rang twice, then went to her voicemail. I hung up, staring at the phone in my hand. Had she declined the call?

The phone gave a buzz as I got a text. It was Chrissy.

I've got a migraine, so I'm going to stay in tonight. Meet for lunch tomorrow? You name the place.

I narrowed my eyes, looking up at the door. Was she really sick with a migraine in her room? Or was she hiding from me? I sighed and tapped out a response on my phone, suggesting a diner in town that we could meet at tomorrow. If she wanted to spend her visit holed up in her room, I wasn't going to stop her.

Cheesy Does It was housed in a bright blue building in the center of town. They served all kinds of dishes, smothered in cheese. They had many options without cheese, but their signature dish was a cheesesteak sandwich with mozzarella sticks on the side. It was probably too cutesy for Chrissy, but I couldn't say no to cheese.

The following afternoon, Chrissy and I met at the front door. I'd spent the morning dealing with vendors on the phone and checking out the last guests who'd stayed with us over the weekend. As the weather cooled, we had fewer families and active guests, and more people looking for quiet and respite from their lives. Wasn't that what Chrissy was doing, too? I pushed that thought away.

At the restaurant's entrance, Chrissy and I ducked under umbrellas and the awning as rain poured down on us. Clouds as far as I could see, and no sign of the rain stopping. Sometimes, I really regretted leaving sunny California for this place.

Dinah, who worked as the hostess and kept her blonde hair piled on top of her head, with ribbons throughout holding it up, led us back to a booth. Cheesy Does It had a fifties vibe inside, with red and white striped booths, an old-fashioned soda fountain in the corner, and classic rock playing on the speakers. Estelle had first introduced me to the place a few weeks ago, and I'd thought it so charming, I had to come back.

"This place is really trying hard to be something it's not, huh?" Chrissy kept her voice down low so Dinah wouldn't hear.

I smirked behind my menu, taking a sip of the water that was already out on the table. As much as she claimed to be open-minded, my sister still had her high standards.

Rain pounded against the windows of the restaurant, creating a cocoon-like feeling around the whole restaurant.

It felt like we were the only people for miles, stuck inside this cheesy place.

It was quiet this afternoon; barely a quarter of the tables had people sitting at them. The rain, plus the weekday, had probably kept many people from coming here for lunch today.

"So what did you get Hannah?" I asked, scanning down the menu. Was I in the mood for a cheesesteak sandwich or a grilled cheese sandwich today? I couldn't go wrong with either.

"What?" Chrissy asked, confusion on her face.

"Hannah. What did you get her?" I set my menu down. "You said you were shopping for souvenirs...?"

"Oh, right." Chrissy gave a short laugh, leaning back in her seat, but she couldn't hide the fact that my question had surprised her. "I couldn't find anything I liked. I'll have to try again tomorrow, I suppose."

How had she forgotten that she'd told me she was getting a gift for her daughter? I hadn't seen her in a day and a half, and she hadn't managed to find *anything* for Hannah? What exactly had she been doing while we were apart?

"Which shops did you try? Maybe I can suggest some-place for you."

"Umm..." Chrissy rubbed her hand against the back of her neck, looking off to the side. "I don't remember what it was called. Porter's, maybe?"

"Did you just make up that name? Never mind. What street was it on?" If she couldn't answer one basic question, maybe she could answer another.

"Oh, look, our server's back!" She straightened up in her seat as Dinah approached from across the room, clearly giving up on lying to me more about her activities since she'd arrived.

"Chrissy, what is going—" I started.

"Ready to order?" Dinah approached our table, interrupting me.

I sighed, but smiled up at Dinah. "I'll have the cheesesteak." Go big or go home, right? If you're going to come to a restaurant with one main special, you may as well eat it, right?

"I'll have a side of mozzarella sticks," Chrissy said, passing her menu to Dinah.

"Anything else?" Dinah asked, scribbling our orders onto her pad.

Chrissy shook her head. "I had a big breakfast," she explained at the look I gave her.

Why would she have a big breakfast if she knew we were meeting for lunch? Also, where had she gone to have breakfast? I hadn't seen her in the bistro that morning, and I didn't remember any big meals being carried up to the rooms.

"Anything to drink?"

"Water's fine," Chrissy and I said at the same time, and we smiled at each other.

"All right, your food will be out in a bit." Dinah took my menu. She left our table, both of us silent at her departure.

Enough was enough. My sister had been acting strange from the moment she arrived, and I was going to get it out of her.

"Chrissy, what is going on?"

"What do you mean?"

"How did you forget you were buying Hannah a souvenir? Where have you been all day? And why are you even in Pine Brook in the first place?" I hissed, dropping my voice low so that people sitting at other tables wouldn't hear me.

Chrissy's eyes widened at my tone, but she dropped her gaze and began fiddling with her napkin. "I don't know what you're talking about. I got distracted and didn't have time to find something for Hannah. I didn't realize me showing up here would be such a hassle for you."

"It's not a hassle, but you have to admit, it's pretty strange. What happened with Mark? Did you two get into a fight or something?"

She looked up at me then, tears brimming in her eyes, but before she had a chance to say anything, two plates of steaming cheese were placed in front of us.

"Enjoy," Dinah said with a wink, leaving us to our food.

Chrissy dug into her mozzarella sticks, keeping her gaze down.

"Everything's fine," she mumbled. "Can we talk about this later?"

I grimaced, but turned to my sandwich. I wasn't going to force her to talk about something she didn't want to in public, especially if it was going to make her cry. But I would make sure we spoke once we got back to her room at the inn. I wanted to help her, but I couldn't do that if I didn't know what was going on.

Twenty minutes later, I leaned back in my seat, remnants of my cheesesteak the only thing left on the plate. Chrissy had finished her mozzarella sticks sooner, and had started talking about work, staring off into the distance as she spoke. I'd let her ramble, content that if she got all of this out now, she'd be more likely to tell me what was really going on later.

"You'd think there'd be less drama with people with PhDs, but honestly, I think it's worse," she said. "It's like we all think we're too smart to be wrong about anything."

"People are people. Drama happens everywhere." I waved over Dinah, who came to take our plates.

"Anything else?" Dinah asked as she cleared the table.

"Just the check."

"Where's the bathroom?" Chrissy asked, glancing around the room.

"In the back. They're actually not part of the main building," Dinah explained. "You have to pass through the patio, and then they are on the right."

"It's quirky." I shrugged, remembering the trek from the last time I was here with Estelle.

I leaned back in my seat as Chrissy left for the bathroom and Dinah carted away our plates. I wanted to get back to the inn soon to make sure everything was running smoothly. Since taking over as owner, I'd become more and more invested in the success of the inn. Any failures or mishaps felt like personal attacks on me. Tracy said I was letting the chaos of the inn affect me too much, but I couldn't help but feel responsible.

A scream pierced the air, and I jumped in my seat. I looked around, trying to identify the sound. It sounded just like...Chrissy!

I bolted out of my seat and went back towards the bathrooms, where she'd been headed. I pushed past a small group of people that had gathered in the tiny hallway, and found Chrissy standing outside. A small alleyway ran between Cheesy Does Its main building and its back patio. Chrissy was standing off to the side in the alleyway, her hands pressed against her face.

I stepped outside, sheets of rain beginning to fall on my face—the awning that covered the patio didn't extend this far out, leading to a gap where we were exposed to the elements. I grabbed Chrissy, checking for wounds or injuries. Her eyes were wide and glazed over, staring right through me. Had she hurt herself somehow?

"What is it? What's wrong?" I held in the urge to shake her when she didn't immediately speak.

She'd dropped her hands by then and was staring at something over my shoulder. I slowly turned around. Pushed up against the wall of the alley, out of sight from the rest of the restaurant, and staring up at us with unseeing eyes, was Elijah's dead body. Blood covered the side of his face, and the green hoodie he'd been wearing the day before was matted with it.

Oh, no. Another murder victim.

5

Dinah took command of the scene, herding us all back into the restaurant and putting in a call to the police. I pulled Chrissy away from the body and held her in my arms as she shook, the impact of what she'd seen coming over her. We followed Dinah back into the restaurant.

As secluded as the alleyway was, I'd gotten a good look at the body from where Chrissy had been standing as we walked back into the restaurant. Instead of taking a right to get to the bathrooms, Chrissy had taken a left before the patio and taken a couple of steps deeper into the alleyway. Had something drawn her attention as she went by?

The alley was long, with dumpsters in the middle. If you were on the street on the other side of the alley, you wouldn't notice the body. With all the rain that morning, none of the patrons at the restaurant would've gone out to the patio. How long had he been back here? And why was Elijah Norris lying murdered behind Cheesy Does It?

Chrissy kept her arms wrapped around me, sniffling into my shirt. I couldn't imagine what it felt like to see your old friend murdered in an alley. He'd been so full of life when we'd seen him the day before. What could I possibly say to Chrissy to reassure her or calm her down?

"Everyone, I need you to remain silent and do exactly what we say." Officer Scott had entered the restaurant and raised his voice to be heard over the murmurings of the crowd. Heads swiveled in his direction as he spoke, any chatter quieting quickly. Two officers rushed out to the back to check on the body, though Elijah wasn't getting up anytime soon.

Officer Scott was young, with sandy blond hair and peach fuzz on his cheeks. His uniform was better fitting than the last time I'd seen him, though his prominent Adam's apple and gangly frame were as I remembered them. He strode over to Dinah, who murmured a few words to him, then she pointed in our direction. I could've sworn Scott physically deflated an inch as he saw me standing there, but he quickly recovered his straight posture, and I couldn't say for sure what I had seen.

Scott spoke to the group gathered inside the restaurant again. "Everyone, please take a seat and remain silent. We'll need to take your statements." His gaze settled on me, and he strode over in our direction as two more officers began talking to the clusters of people scattered about the restaurant.

"I understand you two found the body," he murmured once he was near us. "Please follow me."

I grabbed Chrissy's hand and led her after Officer Scott. Restaurant patrons watched us as we filed past, undoubtedly wondering how I'd managed to stumble onto another dead body in such a short amount of time. I was wondering the same thing, too. Did this many murder victims in less than two months mean I was cursed? Hard to say.

Scott led us through the back door and out to the back patio. Chrissy and I averted our gazes as we passed the alleyway where Elijah's body was still resting. Dinah had cleared out the back patio when calling the police, so the covered outdoor area was quiet. Rain pattered against the roof above us. Scott settled us down at a table, then joined the two other officers at the crime scene area, pulling out his walkie-talkie.

"Is he going to arrest us?" Chrissy whispered.

I reached over and grabbed her hand, giving it a squeeze. "Don't worry. He wants to talk to us because we found the body, but that doesn't mean he'll arrest us. He's just doing his job."

Chrissy let out a sob at the mention of Elijah's body, and I pulled her into my arms again as she cried. I couldn't imagine what she was going through right now. Suddenly seeing Elijah after so long, only for him to show up dead the next day? How terrible that must have been.

But also, was it possibly suspicious? Would Scott think the situation was shadier than it really was? Chrissy suddenly shows up to town, runs into an old friend from years ago, whom she hasn't seen in ages, and then he's dead the next day? Given how evasive Chrissy had been about explaining why she was here, the situation might raise some questions for the police. She wasn't a killer, though; that much, I knew.

The three officers stood around the crime scene. Scott spoke into his walkie-talkie, presumably putting in a call to the medical examiner and letting the station know what had been found. I remembered the protocol from the last crime scene I'd been at. They'd cordon off the area and take all of our statements, while the county medical examiner arrived to give her assessment.

How long had Elijah been back here? Why had no one else stumbled onto his body? It was raining, so people weren't spending time on the outdoor patio, even with the covered awning, but had no one gone to the bathroom yet this morning? The restaurant had been quiet when we'd shown up; maybe no one had needed the bathroom so far today.

Scott finished his discussion with the other two officers and strode back to where we were sitting. "Thanks for your patience. Dinah said you found the body, is that correct?"

"Chrissy did." I gestured to her. "She's my sister, in town for a visit."

Scott turned his attention to her. "I need to ask you some questions about what happened here. Is that all right?"

Chrissy sniffled, but nodded, her face streaked with tears. "Is it okay if Simone stays?"

"Of course. Now, tell me what happened."

As Chrissy took him through the events of the day—coming to lunch, going to the back to use the restroom, finding Elijah's body—I studied Officer Scott. When I'd met him for the first time last month, he'd been green around the gills at the sight of a dead body. While he wasn't completely stoic this time—his Adam's apple bobbed as he swallowed whenever the body came into sight—he'd done an efficient job of taking command of the scene. Those two murders last month had given him some serious experience.

"Why did you take a left back here? The bathroom is to the right," Scott said.

"I didn't realize how much it was raining, so I paused at the door to put on my coat," Chrissy said. "As I did, I glanced to the left and saw something sticking out from behind the dumpster. It looked...weird...so I walked closer. And that's when I saw him." She let out a sob.

It looked *weird*? What about it was so weird?

I needed to stop thinking these thoughts. My sister wasn't a killer. It wasn't suspicious that she didn't have good answers to our questions; it was just what happened when you suddenly found yourself in the middle of a murder investigation. She couldn't have known Elijah was back here, and her emotional reaction seemed genuine. She wasn't some suspect I was trying to catch in a lie.

"Did anyone touch the body or get close to it?" he asked us both.

We shook our heads.

"If you don't mind, can you please hold out your hands?" he asked, gesturing between us. "I need to confirm there's no blood on you."

Chrissy and I dutifully held out our hands, palms down, then flipped them when Scott indicated to do so. He scribbled something down in his notepad.

"I think his name is Elijah Norris," I blurted out into the silence. Scott flicked his eyes up to me, while Chrissy let out a tiny sob next to me. I straightened up in my seat under Scott's gaze. "You'll of course want to confirm with next of kin, but we ran into him at the bistro yesterday. He is—*was* —a tall man. I recognized his hoodie."

"Were you friends with him?"

I shook my head. "Chrissy knows him, from years ago." I snapped my mouth shut. Was I serving up my sister as a potential suspect by mentioning her history with the dead man? The police would figure it out eventually, so it was probably best to be honest now.

Chrissy nodded. "We were in school together years ago. We, ah, ran into each other at the bistro yesterday. You should confirm with next of kin, like Simone said, but I believe that's him." She let out another sob, pressing her hands over her face as she cried.

Officer Scott shifted his weight between his feet, glancing over at me, then back at Chrissy. "We're going to check for I.D., too, once the medical examiner is here. A few more questions, if you don't mind," he said after a moment. Chrissy sniffled and wiped at her cheeks, nodding. "What did you do earlier today, before coming to lunch?"

"I was in town shopping for a souvenir for my daughter," Chrissy said. "She's seven, and I wanted to get her something from my trip."

I tensed at this, though I don't think Scott noticed. When I'd asked Chrissy about the souvenir earlier, she'd seemed to forget that that was what she'd told me she was doing, and she couldn't remember where she'd gone or what the shop was called. But now she was saying that she had been out shopping? Was she trying to say anything to get Scott off her back?

"What did you get her?" Scott asked.

"I couldn't find anything. I'm here for a few days, so I'll probably try again later in the week."

"Did you buy anything today? Talk to anyone at the stores?"

She shook her head. "Like I said, I couldn't find anything I liked. But I'm sure there were cameras in all the stores you could check."

I held in a response, though I knew the answer to that. Pine Brook wasn't exactly up on the latest tech trends, and, even though security cameras had been popular for years now, few stores in town actually used them with any consistency. You were more likely to find a camera with a ten-year-old tape inside, or a store with a camera that only pointed at the cash register. We'd only gotten them at the inn recently, and they barely worked. If Chrissy didn't buy anything or use her credit card, how likely were the police going to be able to confirm her alibi?

Scott turned to me. "And where were you earlier today?"

"At the inn. It was a pretty normal Tuesday for us. Tracy saw me, and so did Hank, and Penny, I think. I'm sure there are others." I'd been through this once before with the police; I wanted to make sure they knew my alibi.

Scott made another note in his notepad. He'd managed to keep his voice level and controlled the whole time he was questioning us, and his hands weren't shaking at all. This was a very different Officer Scott than the one I'd seen at the first murder I'd stumbled onto in Pine Brook. Here, he'd taken command of the scene in a way I hadn't expected. A couple murder investigations had clearly trained him well.

"Ladies, thank you for all of this info. Detective Patel will be by shortly to secure the scene and get the preliminary investigation started. We'll reach out if we have more questions, but you're free to go. If you think of anything else, please get in touch. I'm guessing you'll both be at the Hemlock Inn for the next week?"

Chrissy nodded. "I want to help however I can."

Scott gave us a final nod, then led us back to the restaurant. My eyes automatically drifted over to the crime scene as we passed by. Someone had set up a mini-tent over Elijah's body, presumably to protect it from the elements while they waited for the medical examiner to show up. My stomach turned as I caught a glimpse of his bloody hoodie, and I jerked my attention away from it. Seeing dead bodies never got any easier.

6

Chrissy was quiet on the drive back to the Hemlock. She'd been too shaken up to drive herself back in her rental car, so we agreed to leave it in the restaurant's parking lot, and we'd come pick it up once she'd had a chance to calm down.

What was she thinking about right now? She'd been so emotional once she realized it was Elijah out there; she must still be grappling with those feelings. My sister, the true crime fanatic, who had asked me a million questions the first time I found a dead body, stared out the window into the rain and stayed silent as we drove.

Right as we were turning into the inn's parking lot, she spoke.

"What do you think happened to him?"

I pulled into a parking spot and turned off the engine. "I'm not sure. It looked...bloody. But the police will investigate and figure it out soon, I'm sure. I know the detective on the case. She might be willing to tell me what happened once they have more information."

Chrissy nodded, sniffling. I kept my hands on the

steering wheel, afraid that any sudden movement might spook her.

"He was so young." Her voice was soft. "Only a few years older than me." She turned to me, tears hovering in her eyes. "You don't think I had anything to do with this, right?"

I jerked back in my seat at her words. Where had that come from?

"Why would you say that? You barely knew the guy, right? You're not a murderer."

"I've read enough of these books; I know it looks suspicious. I show up in town, run into an old friend, and suddenly he's dead? The story tells itself!"

I leaned over and gripped her hands as her voice turned hysterical. "I know you didn't do this. You're not a killer. Like I said, I know the detective on this case, and she's good at her job." She had to be, since the chief of police was so bad at his, but I kept that thought to myself. "As long as you're honest with her about what you know, you'll be fine."

Chrissy nodded and took some deep breaths, calming herself down. I squeezed her hands again, keeping my face neutral.

While I did think Detective Patel was good at her job, that didn't mean people weren't wrongly accused of murder in this town. I'd seen it happen when I first got to town and a rich philanthropist had been murdered. Patel did her best, but this sleepy town had a powerful police chief who didn't always make the right decisions. Would that happen here?

"It does make me wonder what happened to him," Chrissy said. "I mean, when we saw him yesterday, he was so vibrant and full of life. What could've happened in only a day?" Her voice trailed off as she stared off to the side, thinking.

I'd been wondering the same thing. As much as I'd

appreciated the calm at the inn after the chaos of a murder investigation last month, another body in Pine Brook raised a lot of questions for me. Elijah had said he lived in Holliston; why was he murdered behind Cheesy Does It? Had he never left Pine Brook after his brunch yesterday? Or did he return for some reason? Who in his life would hate him so much that they'd want to kill him? Had it been an accident? Or was something more sinister going on?

"I think I'd like to lie down," Chrissy said, breaking into my thoughts. "Give Hannah a call. It'd be nice to hear her voice."

"Call your husband, too. He should know what's going on."

She nodded, then we dashed out of the car and up to the inn. The rain was steady, tap-tap-tapping against the inn's roof and the little awning over the front door. Once inside, we stamped our feet out on the doormat and hung up our raincoats. Someone had lit a fire, and a guest sat in one of the armchairs, scrolling through his phone.

"Do you want me to bring you up some tea, or anything?"

Chrissy shook her head. "I think a lie down is all I need." She pulled me into a hug, squeezing tight, then dashed up the stairs.

I watched her go, my thoughts spinning. Now wasn't the time to get caught up in Elijah's death. The police could handle this, and my sister needed my support. I was going to stay out of things as best I could.

"Excuse me? Would you be able to help me?" A woman approached from the staircase, wringing her hands together. She was in her early forties, with long, dark brown hair that hung down to her waist, pale skin, and thick, Coke-bottle glasses that kept slipping down her nose. Her eyes were as wide as saucers as she looked around.

"Of course." I guided her over to the front desk, wracking my brain for a name. She'd just arrived to the Hemlock, and we'd put her in Room 12. What was her name again?

Morgana, that was it, Morgana Byers. I took up my position behind the front desk and straightened a stack of papers piled haphazardly on the counter. Nadia was nowhere to be seen, but she'd managed to leave behind a mess.

"What can I help you with, Ms. Byers?"

"Oh, please, call me Morgana." Her cheeks flushed as she spoke. "Everyone's been so kind here. I wondered if you might be able to recommend a spa in the area?"

"Absolutely." I reached under the desk and pulled out a stack of folded papers. Flipping through them quickly, I removed the brochures which advertised spas, and held them out for Morgana to take a look.

"Holliston is just a short drive away, and has some great spas and beauty centers." I flipped through the first brochure. "You can get a wrap, a massage, and a pedicure, plus they'll even throw in a green smoothie."

Morgana's face scrunched up. "Oh, I've never much liked those green smoothies. Makes me think I'm drinking grass!"

"Don't tell anyone, but I feel the same way," I said with a wink. "If you're not into green smoothies, the Sound View Spa is completely unpretentious and lets you watch Netflix while you relax. It's about a thirty-minute drive, and has lovely views of, well, the Puget Sound, hence the name."

Morgana grinned widely and took the brochure, flipping through the pages. "This is wonderful. I could use a little Netflix viewing. I do so love your town. It's my first time in

Pine Brook, but I definitely want to come back. Any chance of opening a spa here at the inn?"

"Oh, my, we definitely don't have the space for that," I said with a laugh, though, even as I spoke, I thought of all the space in the back of the inn that was currently shrubs and greenery. Could a spa fit back there? We'd have to do some major remodeling to make it happen, but it wasn't the wildest idea we'd ever had.

"Well, I'm absolutely going to tell all my friends about this place. If you ever open a spa, let me know!"

"What brings you to town?" I asked, sorting the remaining brochures back into a pile and slipping them under the desk.

"My in-laws are in town," she said, dropping her voice a level, as if her in-laws were hiding around the corner. "My husband and I live in Portland, and I had to get away for a couple of days."

"Well, we're very happy to have you here for a bit. I can promise you'll be safe from any stressful in-laws at that spa!"

"Fantastic." Morgana's smile had lit up her face, true joy flashing across her features as she envisioned her trip to the spa.

"Let us know if you need anything else," I called as she waved goodbye and left the front desk. I smiled as she walked away. Life at the Hemlock Inn could be hectic, but I loved the opportunity to help guests find something truly special during their stay here.

I turned my attention back to the front desk, straightening up the piles left behind by Nadia—not everything here was glamorous and fun, unfortunately—but was interrupted by a speeding bullet. Well, it was Estelle, but sometimes she felt like a speeding bullet when she came out of nowhere.

"Simone! There you are! Is it true you found another dead body?" she asked, not making any effort to keep her voice quiet.

I whipped my head around to see if anyone had heard her, but the lobby was quiet. I grabbed Estelle's arm and pulled her out to the courtyard. I wanted to update her on what was happening, but we didn't need to do it out in the open like this.

The courtyard was in the center part of the inn, and all the rooms and sitting areas branched off from it. Unlike most fully open-air courtyards, Sylvia and Tracy had made sure to add a glass ceiling because of the Washington weather.

Rain tapped against the glass, and the air was cooler out here, but we were alone, and it was quiet. I turned to Estelle, who was bouncing up and down on her heels, her eyes wide. Why did I keep hanging around people so obsessed with murder?

"It's true," I said. "Well, technically Chrissy found him. He was in the back alley of Cheesy Does It."

"Do you know who it was?" Estelle asked.

I hesitated. Officer Scott had said they were going to find Elijah's next of kin to identify his body. I didn't want to go blabbing around town that I'd found his body before his family could be told.

"I think they're still trying to identify him." This was technically true, since his family should be the one to confirm his death. "I'm sure they'll say something soon."

Estelle nodded, the wheels in her head turning. "I'm sure you're right. I can probably ask Miriam if she knows anything."

Estelle's hair dresser's mother, Miriam, worked at the front desk at the police station and shouldn't have had access to the things she did, but sometimes managed to get us the information we needed.

"I can't believe you found another body," Estelle went on. "And with your sister in town! You must attract bad luck or something."

"I wouldn't say that. I think this town has more murder than we realize." Or was Estelle right, and I was haunted, destined to be followed around by murder victims for eternity? A chill went through me at the thought.

"Maybe you're right," Estelle said with a shrug, not seeming to notice that I was spooked. "Still, it's pretty exciting. Are we going to catch the killer again?"

"No!" I said sternly with a shake of my head. "We got lucky last time, but we can't get involved in another murder investigation. It's not safe! We need to leave this to Detective Patel and the police."

"You're probably right. Still, maybe they'll need some help again. I'll go give Miriam a call." Estelle fled the courtyard before I could talk her out of it, pulling out her cell phone and dialing her friend.

I wasn't interested in getting involved with Elijah's death, but I knew I wouldn't be able to stop Estelle from poking around, so I left her to it.

Instead, I stopped at the front desk to check in with Tracy. I hadn't had a chance to talk to her all day, and this was rapidly turning into a day where I needed her candor and normalcy to keep me grounded. I wasn't haunted, no matter what Estelle thought.

Only a month ago, Tracy and I had avoided each other, as our conversations always seemed to lead to bickering. Now, she was the person I went to when I wanted to complain about a vendor or talk about the cute thing that

Lola did that night. Aunt Sylvia hadn't just left me an inn; she'd left me a friend, too.

As I approached the front desk, Lola crawled out of her bed from behind the desk and came looking for some pats. I ruffled her ears and passed her a dog treat from the bin we kept in a drawer. I slipped behind the desk and began sorting through the mail that had piled up on the counter.

"Look what I found in the storage closet," Tracy said, pulling something up onto the front desk. She held up a silver teapot with a curved spout and etchings along the handle. It was tarnished in some places but looked fancy enough.

"I can't tell how old it is, but it could be really old, right?" Tracy asked, holding the teapot up into the air and studying its underside.

I held in a chuckle at the sight of her paying such close attention to a kitchen appliance.

"Maybe," I said, leafing through the mail. Junk, junk, and more junk, with some bills thrown in for good measure. Ah, the life of a small business owner.

Tracy set the teapot back underneath the desk and turned her attention to our ledger opened on the desk in front of her. She bent her head and started tallying up the numbers for the day.

"How's your sister doing? I heard about what happened at Cheesy Does It. You really need to stop finding all these dead bodies."

I held in a groan and tossed the junk mail into the recycling bin under the desk. Gossip sure traveled fast in this town.

"Chrissy is okay," I said, focusing on the first part of her question. "She's upstairs now. I think what she saw today really scared her. She knew the guy; did I tell you that?

Apparently, they know each other from way back. It seems like an odd coincidence that they'd both be at the inn on the same day. He said he was here for brunch, but it's strange. And then the next day, he's dead in town."

Tracy shrugged, still counting numbers in her head. I never knew how she could do math and have a conversation at the same time. I had to lock myself in the office with a white noise machine blaring in order to focus on the sums in front of me.

"It's not so crazy. This is a popular inn."

"Maybe you're right," I said, my mind running over the events of the day.

I'd been so busy dealing with the inn after we ran into Elijah at the bistro yesterday that I hadn't thought much about what it meant for Elijah to be here. But now that he was dead, it changed things.

"Something weird did happen," I said slowly.

Tracy flicked her eyes up to me, then straightened at my perplexed expression. "What? Besides the dead body?"

We were alone in the lobby—that guest who'd been reading at the fireplace had gone into the bistro—and I trusted Tracy to keep her mouth shut about things. Tracy had good instincts about these kinds of things, and I wanted her opinion.

I took a step closer to her, lowering my voice. "I think Chrissy lied to the police. They asked where she was today, and she said she'd been shopping for a souvenir for her daughter."

"So? That seems plausible."

"Except when I asked her what she was doing, she said she hadn't bought Hannah anything, and she'd even forgotten that she had said she was going shopping. I don't think she was doing that today at all. Why would she lie to the police about it?"

Tracy shrugged, though the serious look in her eyes betrayed her attempt at nonchalance. "Maybe she did a little shopping and told the police that because it was easiest. When the cops ask you for an alibi, it's best to have one."

We'd both learned that firsthand last month. Still, it didn't explain what Chrissy had actually been doing today. Had she gone to see Elijah and then lied to me about it?

7

"**H**ow'd you sleep?"

Chrissy shifted in her seat across from me, her head down and focused on her bowl of oatmeal. "The bed was really soft."

Dark circles still framed her eyes. She poked at her oatmeal but didn't take a bite.

It was the next morning, and we'd met for breakfast in the bistro. Chrissy had suggested it when I'd figured she'd want to stay in bed all day. I wasn't going to force her to stay inside, though.

Chrissy had been too tired the day before to go pick up her rental car, so Tracy had given me a ride to Cheesy Does It later in the evening so that I could pick up Chrissy's car. Crime scene tape was strung up around the front of the restaurant, and I'd averted my gaze as I hurried to Chrissy's rental.

"That's not really an answer." Back at the bistro, I leaned forward and lowered my voice. "Are you sure you want to eat here right now? Like I said, I can bring breakfast up to your room."

She looked up and smiled, though it seemed forced. "I wanted to get out of the room. It's fine. I can't stay hidden away forever, can I?"

"No, I guess not." I couldn't imagine what she was going through, having discovered the dead body of an old friend. It was enough to make anyone break down, but my sister was strong.

"I still can't believe that was Elijah. I wonder what had been going on in his life to lead to his violent death like that." Her voice was thoughtful, though it still held a tremor of sadness.

"Do you know anything about his personal life? Was he married, or did he have kids? I'm sure the police have looked into this already, but it might help to remember in case they ask."

"He was married after grad school, but I think they may have gotten a divorce a couple of years ago. I don't know much about it, of course, but I think I saw some mention of it on Facebook at some point. No kids, though."

I didn't begrudge Patel having to break the news to the man's ex-wife. Although, if you were an ex-wife, did you have the same feelings about your former husband? Having never been married, I couldn't say for sure, but it seemed reasonable that the feelings that had led to you getting married wouldn't simply go away because of a divorce.

"Listen, I think we should talk about what happened yesterday." I kept my voice low, though there weren't many other people in the bistro today. We'd managed to miss the breakfast rush, and things wouldn't pick up until lunch. Right now, we needed to stop dancing around the topic. "Did you know Elijah was going to be at the inn? Is that why you came to Washington?"

Chrissy's mouth dropped open and her eyes widened. "What? No, of course not. That's absurd. It was purely coincidence. I came here to see you, remember?"

"I don't mean to accuse you of anything, but you have to understand how this looks to the police. They're probably going to have more questions for you. The detective on the case, Patel? She's good at her job, and she won't stop digging for the truth. You need to be prepared for what they find out. I need you to be honest with me about what you're really doing here. I can't help you if you aren't honest with me."

I'd been up half the night thinking about it. I believed my sister wasn't a killer, but her actions since she'd gotten to town had been suspicious. Surprising me with this visit and not giving a straight answer when I pressed her on it, running into an old friend at my bistro, not being honest about where she was all day, and then finding that same friend's dead body the next day—the police were bound to think more was going on here than Chrissy was letting on.

Of course, it could have all been innocent. But that was why I needed the truth from Chrissy. What was the point in lying, if she hadn't done anything wrong?

"I already told you, I don't know why Elijah was here. And I don't know anything about who killed him." She sat back in her seat with a sigh, hanging her head. "I'm sorry if I've been acting weird. I know I surprised you with this visit. I probably should've called first. It's just...things with Mark haven't been good recently. We got into a huge fight last week, and I needed to get away." She looked up at me then, her eyes brimming with tears. "I didn't have anything to do with Elijah's death. You have to believe me."

"Of course I believe you." I reached out and grabbed her

hands, giving them a squeeze. She pulled a tissue out of her pocket and dabbed at her eyes.

So, something had happened at home that had driven her up here. What was this fight with Mark about? Why hadn't she told me the truth sooner? I still had so many questions, but we weren't alone right now, and I didn't want to make her cry even more. She'd have to tell me eventually, right?

"Simone, someone's here to see you." Nadia had entered the bistro and come over to our table. Chrissy hurriedly wiped at her face.

"Who is it?" I turned in my seat to find Detective Patel standing in the doorway.

"Actually," she said, striding over to our table, "this has to do with Chrissy, too. Why don't we step outside for a moment?"

Chrissy gulped. Police questioning was not top of the list of things either of us wanted to do today, but it was best if we went along with it.

Chrissy and I followed Patel out of the bistro. Penny and Eddy, another server, watched from the side, and Eddy squeezed my hand as we went past. The lobby was quiet, and I led us over to the front desk.

"We found prints at the crime scene that we can't iden-tify, so we'd like to take a set from you to try to eliminate yours," Patel said to Chrissy once we were alone. "It shouldn't take long. Can you come down to the station now?"

"Can't you take the prints here?" I asked. "Why do we need to go all the way to the station?"

Patel shook her head. "Unfortunately, it needs to happen at the station. I also wanted to go over your statement and make sure we have all the details correct. You're both welcome to come."

Chrissy and I exchanged a glance. This didn't seem like the time to argue with Patel about what we should and shouldn't do, so we grabbed our jackets and followed her outside.

Chrissy grabbed my arm as we left the building, slowing us down. "Do you think I need a lawyer for this?" she whispered. "Oh, if only Mark were here! He'd know what to do."

"It's okay," I murmured, shushing her. Patel was a few feet ahead of us, and hadn't appeared to hear anything. "I know someone in town we can call if it seems like you should have an attorney. All they want to do right now is check your fingerprints and confirm your statement. We'll be fine."

I gulped as we followed after Patel, hoping that was true.

The police station was a squat, drab building located downtown. Patel kept to the speed limit as she drove, and we kept close behind her in my car. Chrissy stared out the window, her hands clenched in her lap.

I parked in the public lot, and we followed Patel into the building. She led us through the back offices, to a small room with an ink pad set up for taking prints. I'd had to do this once before, so my prints were already on file with the department. Chrissy followed Patel's instructions, then we followed the detective to another room, this one with a couch and vending machine.

"A snack? Anything to drink?" Patel asked as we settled onto the couch.

We shook our heads.

She took a seat in a chair across from us and pulled out her notepad. "Thanks again for coming down. Like I said, I need to go over your statement and make sure we have all the right details."

She led Chrissy through the same line of questioning Officer Scott had taken her through the day before, though the questions were in a different order and phrased slightly differently. It was almost like she was checking to see if Chrissy's story stayed consistent. I kept my mouth shut, not wanting to seem like I was trying to insert myself into something I shouldn't be a part of.

"Were you involved with the victim?" Patel asked.

"Involved?" Chrissy reared back in her seat.

"Involved how?" I asked.

Patel flicked her gaze over to me. "Romantically."

"No." Chrissy shifted in her seat. "I'm a married woman."

Patel flipped through to an earlier page in her notepad and began reading from her notes. "When we ran an online search of Elijah Norris, we found old social media posts featuring you. We're guessing this was while you were in graduate school together. You were in a relationship, weren't you?"

Chrissy deflated beside me, hanging her head. "Yes. It...it was years ago, though. It has nothing to do with what happened to Elijah yesterday."

I kept my mouth shut, as I didn't want to make things worse for Chrissy, but my thoughts were all in a jumble. She'd just lied to the police about her relationship with a murder victim, *and* been immediately caught in the lie. That was not a good look for her. Why was she lying about their past? What else was she lying about?

Patel made a note to herself. "Why did you break up?"

"The same reason anyone in graduate school breaks up. When we were done, we were headed to different jobs.

Elijah came to Washington, and I went back home to L.A. and got my job at a university down there."

"How long were you together?"

"A couple of years. It wasn't all that serious. We both knew we probably wouldn't end up in the same place once school was done, as our fields of study were different."

"I thought you were both sociology professors." Patel paused her note taking, confusion on her face.

"We are. I mean, we were. But Elijah was more focused on quantitative research, crunching numbers and all that, while I was focused on the qualitative, more anthropological side of the discipline. Focus areas like that change over the years, of course, and I'm not doing the exact same thing I was then, but at the time, our focus areas led us in different directions. After grad school, it made sense to part ways. Had we stayed in the same place, things might've been different, but life doesn't always go the way you planned, right?"

Her voice had turned wistful as she talked about their past relationship. Was she...*sad* that they weren't together anymore? Or was she simply upset because an old friend was murdered? I didn't know what to trust anymore.

"Can you account for your whereabouts yesterday between 10:30 a.m. and noon?" Patel asked.

"Of course she can," I interjected. "I'm guessing that's when Elijah was killed? Go ahead, Chrissy, tell her where you were." This whole line of questioning was insane, and I wasn't going to let Patel try to pin a murder on my sister.

Chrissy looked up at me, tears streaming down her face. "Simone, I'm so sorry for lying. I should've told you about our past sooner."

"Please focus," Patel cut in. "Where were you between 10:30 a.m. and noon yesterday?"

Chrissy looked at Patel. "I don't know. I was driving around. I...I don't think anyone saw me."

Patel stood. "I need to take you back to one of our interview rooms. You need to stay out here," she added to me. Chrissy stood and followed her out of the room.

"Wait! I don't understand. Why are you doing this?" I asked, following after the two of them.

Another officer was standing outside the room, and Patel passed Chrissy over to him. He led Chrissy away, and Patel turned to me.

"Your sister doesn't have an alibi for the time of the murder, and she was in a relationship with the murder victim that she lied to us about. We need to ask her some more questions, and you can't be there for that. Now, please, let us do our job."

"Does she need a lawyer?" I couldn't let Chrissy get arrested for something she didn't do!

Patel paused. "She's not under arrest...but it might be a good idea to find her an attorney." With that, she strode away, leaving me to stare after them.

I CALLED the only lawyer I knew in town, and, twenty minutes later, Ron met me at the station.

"How is she?" he asked, joining me in the lobby.

"Pretty shaken up, I think. But I haven't heard anything yet."

Ron spoke to the officer sitting at the front desk. Their voices were too low for me to hear anything useful. After a moment, Ron came back.

"They're going to let me speak with her. I'll be back in a few minutes."

I sat in one of the chairs in the lobby and waited for Ron to return. Forty minutes later, he came through the doors with Chrissy in tow. I sprung up and pulled her into a hug. Ron led us out of the station.

"What happened in there?" I asked once we were away from prying ears. "Do they think you had something to do with Elijah's death?"

Ron spoke for Chrissy, who looked shell-shocked from everything that had happened.

"They have their suspicions, but they are lacking hard proof," he said. "I imagine they'll keep investigating until they find something that confirms what they believe. They did mention they'd like to take a look at your sister's rental car and run some tests on the exterior. I would make sure you cooperate with whatever they need."

A shiver coursed through me at his words. Why were they testing her rental car? Was Elijah killed by a car?

"You two should go back to the inn and lie low until we have more information," Ron went on. "I'll see what I can find out on my end."

"Thanks for all your help, Ron," I said. I led Chrissy back to my car and we drove away from the police station.

"Are you okay?" I asked after a few moments of silence. "What did they say to you in there?"

"Isn't it obvious? They think I killed him. Why did I come here in the first place? This is all turning into such a big mess."

"Why didn't you tell me you'd been in a relationship with Elijah?"

"I didn't want you to think anything was wrong, and I knew you'd get suspicious if I told you about it. But I didn't kill him, I promise you that."

"I believe you." What else could I say? I wanted to do

what I could to keep Chrissy safe. I wasn't going to let the police arrest her for something she didn't do, no matter how suspicious it might have seemed.

8

"You know I didn't kill him, right?"

"Of course I know that." She'd already asked me that question once, but clearly it was still weighing on her.

Chrissy and I had returned to the inn and were hanging up our coats in the lobby. A fire was crackling in the fireplace, and the smell of something tasty coming from the bistro hung in the air.

"Well, what are you going to do about it?" Chrissy turned to me with her hands on her hips.

"What do you mean?"

"You've solved one murder already in this town. Can't you solve another? I can't go to jail."

"We shouldn't get ahead of ourselves. The police don't have anything on you yet. Let's take Ron's advice and lie low, and see what they have to say after a couple of days."

Chrissy let out a huff. "You better hope I don't get arrested." She turned on her heel and stomped away to the stairs.

An hour later, I was typing away at the computer in my office, trying to distract myself from everything that was going on. Chrissy hadn't come down from her room, so I'd grabbed lunch from the bistro and brought it back to the office to try to get some work done. I picked at a salad on the plate, staring at the computer screen. I had several emails that I needed to work my way through answering, but all I could think about was Elijah and who had killed him.

Was Chrissy right, and I should try to find his killer? Or was she trying to cover her bases after lying to the police about their past together?

Without thinking it through, I pulled up Google and typed in Elijah's name. After a couple of searches, I found his Facebook page. His settings weren't set to private, so I was able to see most of his page.

News of his death had landed on Facebook, and the last few postings were all condolences and nice messages about what a great teacher and friend he was. I clicked on some of the profiles of the people who had commented and saw that it appeared to be a mix of students and other professors.

I scrolled through Elijah's photos. Mostly pictures of his food, him standing on nice vistas, occasionally with a woman under his arm, but mostly he was alone. Until about three years ago; before that point, the majority of his photos were either him with a beautiful woman standing next to him, or the beautiful woman by herself, with sappy captions like, "Love of my life!" and "Get you a girl who can cook and talk Freud!" I rolled my eyes and kept scrolling.

The woman in the photos was a few inches shorter than Elijah, with long blonde hair that curled at the ends. She had a pretty face, round with pink cheeks. Her eyes glittered as she stared up at the camera or into Elijah's eyes. I hovered my mouse over one of the photos, and her tag popped up: Kristina Rohl. Was this the ex-wife Chrissy had told me about? She wasn't in his recent photos, but she was all over his page a few years ago.

I clicked over to her profile and raised my eyebrows as her photos loaded. Much had changed in three years. In the few photos I could see, her hair was cut short and she'd lost some weight. Her captions were vague, the kind of annoying dither I always hated about social media: "Don't let anyone tell you your worth" and "If people really cared, don't you think they'd tell you?"

It looked like she had previously worked at Holliston College, though now her job was simply "freelancer." What did that mean? I scrolled back through some of her photos, but her privacy settings were stronger than Elijah's, and I didn't get very far.

If this was the ex-wife Chrissy had told me about, it looked like she had gone through quite a transformation after their divorce. Did she still live in Holliston? It was hard to tell from her photos. If I was going to investigate Elijah's death, she would be a good person to talk to next. But, I reminded myself, I wasn't investigating Elijah's death. I was leaving that up to the police, like a good citizen.

I sighed and closed out Facebook, turning back to the unread emails, but I couldn't focus. A man was dead, and my sister was a suspect. How could I be expected to get anything done when the threat of jail time for Chrissy was still very real? She wasn't a killer, but unless the police found another suspect, she would be in trouble.

∼

THIRTY MINUTES LATER, I rang the doorbell to Estelle and Miles' home. I couldn't get Elijah's murder out of my head, and I wanted to feel like I was doing something to help

Chrissy. These two were probably also thinking about the murder, too.

Miles answered the door and led me back to the kitchen, where Estelle was rolling cookie dough into balls. The room smelled of sugar and icing.

"There's tea in there," Estelle said by way of greeting, gesturing to a teapot sitting on the counter. "Help yourself."

Miles pulled out a mug for me, and I poured myself a cup. I leaned against the counter watching Estelle bake, while Miles puttered around, sweeping up the flour and sugar that Estelle scattered onto the floor as she worked. It was like these two could read each other's minds. They were of similar height, with the same gray hair on top, making them seem almost like siblings. However, Miles' round, dreamy face and Estelle's quick wit and bright lipstick made them stand apart under further inspection.

"What are you going to do about Elijah's death?" Estelle asked, placing the balls of dough onto cookie sheets.

"Who said anything about Elijah's death?" I asked.

She rolled her eyes. "Don't play coy with me. You don't solve one murder—two, in fact—and then not solve another one that pops up. I can tell that's what you're thinking."

Estelle seemed to have a knack for reading my mind. "You're exactly right. I don't know what it is, but I feel compelled to get involved again. The police think Chrissy is lying about her alibi. I'm worried they're going to arrest her for something she didn't do."

"And you can't stay away from a murder investigation," Miles added with a playful grin. "Don't try to deny it. We can see the wheels spinning in your head as we speak."

He was right. I couldn't get it out of my head. Why was Elijah killed in Pine Brook? Had someone followed him here from Holliston and finished him off? How had he died?

The police wanted to test the exterior of Chrissy's car, so did that mean he was run over by a car? He was a big man; it probably would have taken something pretty strong to overpower him.

"Let's say you're right. What would I even do about it? I don't know where to start. Elijah wasn't from here, so who would talk to me about him?"

"I'm not sure," Estelle admitted with a shrug. "I asked Miriam at the station for more details, but I guess she got in trouble last month for sharing so much with me, and she was worried about her job. She's sixty-eight, for goodness' sake. She should learn to take a risk once in a while. But we can't all be daring."

I suppressed a laugh and took a sip of tea. Estelle's standards for others were pretty hard to meet. She was daring, all right; she'd been about to go sky-diving when I'd shown up to town the month before, and she'd helped me sneak into the apartment building of one of our suspects during our last murder investigation. Of course, she'd immediately bolted out of the building when someone had asked us what we were doing there, so she wasn't exactly Batman.

"That's fine. I don't want Miriam to lose her job. What about Elijah's job in Holliston? Do you know anything about the college?"

"Not really. Most of my contacts are local."

"Why don't you go straight to his department?" Miles piped up. "Maybe they'll let you into his office if you make up an excuse for why you're there. You might be able to find some reason for why someone would want to kill him."

That wasn't a bad idea. Miles wasn't likely to suggest doing something that involved lying, but sometimes, the best ideas came from the most surprising places.

"I'll head over first thing in the morning." I paused,

waiting for one of them to leap into the silence, though they didn't say anything. "I'm guessing you'll both want to come with me?" They'd been eager to tag along on the last investigation, especially Estelle, even if she had ended up abandoning me at the first sign of danger.

"Don't sound too excited about it," Miles said, his brown eyes twinkling with glee. Though he always looked like he'd misplaced something, and his round eyes made me think I was staring into the face of an inquisitive owl half the time, he had a hidden sense of humor that always tickled me.

"It's probably best if you go on your own," Estelle said, smiling and slipping the cookie sheet into the oven. "We don't want too many people hanging around. It might look suspicious. I'll go talk to Miriam tomorrow and try to convince her to share more about Elijah's case. She's bound to share something once I threaten to tell everyone she uses pre-made pie crusts in her signature pie dish. She thinks no one knows, but I can tell," she added with a sniff.

"Sounds good," I said, hoping that I never made Estelle angry enough that she decided to hold something against me.

"Oh, dear. It seems I've made a mess of things."

Estelle and I turned to Miles, and I burst out laughing at the sight of him. He'd been carrying a bag of flour from the counter to the pantry, and somehow had spilled the entire bag all over himself. He looked up at us, his face and clothes covered in white powder, his eyes wide and frantic, and coughed as he inhaled flour.

"Honey, how did this happen?" Estelle hurried over to his side, grabbing a cloth from the kitchen sink. She was going to need a much bigger towel.

The oven timer dinged, and Estelle gestured to a pair of oven mitts on the counter. "Would you mind getting those?"

"Of course." I slipped on the mitts and pulled out a different tray of cookies from the oven. "I think I should let you two handle all this," I added, waving my hand in their general direction. "I'll let you know if I find anything at the college."

"Be safe," Estelle said, wiping down Miles' cheeks with the cloth.

I grabbed a cookie off the sheet as I left the kitchen, quickly shoving it into my mouth before Estelle could stop me.

"I will," I called over my shoulder, my mouth burning from the cookie. Oh well, it was worth it. Estelle could make an impressive chocolate chip cookie.

9

The next morning, I tapped my fingers on the steering wheel in time with the music on the radio as I made my way out of Pine Brook and headed in the direction of Holliston. Penny had called in sick that morning, so I'd helped Eddy in the bistro, serving breakfast and chatting with guests, before heading out for the college.

The song on the radio ended, and it switched over to the host.

"This is always a sad one to have to report," the man on the radio said. "A man was found killed in the small town of Pine Brook, just north of Holliston College. Police are keeping quiet about their investigation, though sources say a former girlfriend is a person of interest."

I turned up the volume, hoping to get more information about the police's investigation.

"In other news, Gerald the turkey has escaped the turkey pasture he was relocated to and returned to the Holliston neighborhood where he was first found. Residents say they don't mind putting up with their new turkey mascot."

I rolled my eyes and switched off the radio. Apparently,

this guy was more interested in the antics of a turkey than reporting on an actual crime. People talked about how short our attention spans were getting when it came to the news, but jeez, this was pretty bad. Still, I did appreciate hearing about Gerald's escapades around town.

I'd checked on Chrissy that morning before heading out, and she'd looked like she hadn't slept well again.

"I know I said that we should let the police handle the investigation, but I can't sit around while they try to build a case against you." We were sitting on her bed, and I reached out and squeezed her shoulder.

Chrissy's eyes lit up at my words. "What are you going to do first? Can I come with you?"

"Slow down, Nancy Drew. I'm going to check out the college Elijah worked at this morning. See if I can sneak into his office, or maybe talk to someone who worked with him."

Chrissy smirked. "Right, and *I'm* the one acting like Nancy Drew, while you talk about breaking into college campuses. This sounds dangerous—I should probably come with you."

I rolled my eyes. "It's a college campus, not Fort Knox. I'll be fine."

"I just want to clear my name as soon as I can. Besides, Elijah's killer should be sitting in jail right now. I'd like to help find the person who did this."

"I get that, I really do. I'll keep you in the loop on what I find. Remember what Ron said about lying low? Besides, it might be suspicious if multiple people show up to the college. It's better if I go alone."

"You're right, you're right. I'll hang out here. Check in with me when you get back, though. I want to hear all about what you find out!"

She couldn't keep the glee out of her voice. My sister, the

true crime fan, had finally found herself smack dab in the middle of a murder investigation. Obviously she wouldn't be this happy if the police arrested her, so I needed to find them another suspect.

Traffic was light as I drove, and I made it to campus in record time. I hadn't spent much time in Holliston since moving to Pine Brook. I knew it was a larger, more diverse town, mainly because of the college that brought in students from all over the country. Holliston College was considered a liberal arts gem, attracting many eager students and wealthy donors.

The rain had stopped and the sun had emerged, though it was chilly outside. I parked my car in front of the sociology department and climbed out, grabbing a wool cap from the back seat—a gift from Tracy, who was convinced I wouldn't be able to handle the freezing temperatures as the winter season wore on. I pulled the cap down over my ears and burrowed my hands into my pockets, grateful for the warmth, and strode to the front doors of the department.

Once inside, I followed signs pointing me to the front desk. The halls were quiet; class must have been in session. A woman sat behind the front desk, her head bent as she typed away on her keyboard. She was in her forties, her dark hair pulled back into a severe bun, with streaks of gray flashing throughout. A pair of wire-rimmed glasses sat perched on the end of her nose. Her face was powered, like she used a heavy hand when applying makeup in the morning.

Her eyes sagged with complete exhaustion. This was a woman who hadn't been sleeping much lately and used her makeup as armor to face the world. I straightened my posture and raised my chin up, wanting to convey a sense of authority in front of this woman who probably dealt with whining undergrads all day.

"Can I help you?" she asked, her voice stern and no-nonsense. I guessed she was some kind of administrator. Would she be likely to talk to me about Elijah?

"I'm looking for Professor Norris," I said, shifting my weight between my feet. "I understand he works in this department?"

The woman sighed and removed her glasses, pressing her fingertips against her eyes as if to ward off a headache. A dead professor probably led to a lot of logistical problems, which in turn would cause a headache for someone in charge of the running of the department.

"Unfortunately, Professor Norris is unavailable right now," she said, her voice devoid of any emotion. "What business do you have with him? We might have another professor you can speak with."

"Unavailable" was an interesting choice of words. Was that what the department was telling everyone about Elijah? Did the students even know that he was dead?

Another voice cut through the quiet building. "Lisa, do we have a problem here?"

A man had stepped out of one of the offices lining the hallway, and he approached the front desk. I took a step back, overwhelmed by his good looks and his sandalwood cologne.

He was tall, probably around six feet, with flowing dark brown hair pushed back from his head, intense brown eyes, and two dimples in his cheeks that wouldn't go away, even when he frowned, which he was doing now. His tweed coat and bowtie had visions of pipes and stern lecturers dancing through my head.

"I'm looking for Professor Norris," I managed to sputter out. "Is he not here right now?"

The man in front of me softened at Elijah's name. "I'll handle this," he said to Lisa, then turned back to me and slipped his hand under my elbow, guiding me away from the front desk.

Normally, someone grabbing my arm like this would cause me to jerk away and maybe hit something in response, but instead I found myself leaning into his strong embrace and had to pinch my arm to focus. Just because he looked like Cary Grant didn't mean I needed to go all googly-eyed.

"Sorry for Lisa's defensiveness," he said once we were a few feet away from the front desk. "The department still hasn't figured out exactly how to communicate the news to the larger community. I take it you haven't heard?"

"Heard what?" I asked, feigning innocence. In for a penny, in for a pound, right? Deception during a murder investigation was part of the deal.

The man sighed. "I thought so. Why don't we step into my office for a moment?"

He gestured to an open door I hadn't realized we were standing in front of, and I stepped into the room. He slipped in behind me and shut the door part of the way, though he kept it somewhat open. Maybe he was hoping that if I burst into tears at the news of Elijah's death, he could easily call for help and get me out of his office.

"I'm Quincy Martell." He motioned for me to take a seat and settled himself behind the desk.

The office was spacious and well lit. Two windows against the far wall let in some of the sunshine from outside, and I spotted a couple mugs of coffee on his desk.

"I'm Si-Samantha," I sputtered, the lie out of my mouth before I realized what I was doing. If this man decided to tell the police that someone had been by asking questions about Elijah, hopefully Detective Patel wouldn't realize I was butting my head in where it didn't belong.

"I'm an old friend of Elijah's," I went on. "Did something happen?"

Quincy took a deep breath, pinching the bridge of his nose between two fingers. "I'm sorry to have to tell you this, but Elijah is dead."

A beat passed between us as his words washed over me. An old friend of Elijah's would probably be upset by this news, so I let out a gasp.

"Are you serious? I don't believe this. I haven't seen him in years, but he was so young. Was he sick? What happened?"

Quincy shrugged. "I'm not sure. Apparently, he was found a couple towns over. The police have been by, but they wouldn't say much. Just taped off his office and took a few items. I don't get the sense it was an illness, though. They said he'd been attacked. We're all so upset by the news."

As he spoke, he sat up a little straighter in his seat, and a gleam appeared in his eye. Was he...relishing the drama that a murder investigation brought to his college? He'd rushed to my side at the front desk when he realized I didn't know about Elijah's death and that he could tell me, and he'd herded me into his office, where he could play the expert and console me. Or was this simply him being a caring professor, and I was too suspicious of people?

"Have you worked with Elijah long?" I asked.

"Oh, years." Quincy leaned back into his chair. "I honestly couldn't tell you who got here first. He was a good professor and a great colleague."

"What did the police ask when they were here? Do they think he was killed, or something?"

Quincy shrugged. "I'm not sure. They didn't say much about what they were thinking. How did you say you knew him?"

"Oh, we were in grad school together years ago. I'm in town for...work, and when I realized Elijah taught at this college, I thought I'd look him up."

"Oh, are you still in academia?" Quincy leaned forward in his seat. "What college do you work at?"

My mind went blank. Drat. This is what I got for lying—having to quickly come up with another lie on the spot. This sleuthing business was much harder than I gave it credit for.

"No, I got out of academia years ago. I'm in the private sector now, in...hospitality...research." The words dropped out of my mouth like stones, heavy and forced out of my brain. The lie rang out through the room, as obvious as if I'd given Quincy a wink and a nudge, but he nodded, his gaze unwavering.

"Interesting. Well, I'm sorry this is what your trip has turned into. I can't imagine what you're going through right now." His features shifted into a compassionate look, but his eyes still held their original intensity. Why did it feel like this man was going through the motions of being sympathetic, without actually feeling that way?

"Yes, it's all such a shock. I had no clue I'd find this. What do you think happened to him?"

"I wish I knew. Were you two close?"

I raised my eyebrows at his sudden turn of questioning but adjusted quickly and came up with another lie. Why was he so focused on me? Was he suspicious about the sudden arrival of Elijah's old "friend" so soon after his death?

"We'd grown apart in recent years because of the distance—I live in Los Angeles—but we'd been close once before. I'd been hoping to rekindle our friendship on this trip. I'm so surprised by this news."

Quincy leaned in and dropped his voice, flicking his eyes up to the door. Was he afraid someone outside would hear him?

"Yes, we were all surprised here, too. Elijah was a great professor, loved by all his students and everyone in the department...but I'm not surprised he's dead. He'd been acting...erratically the past few months. Missing classes and forgetting his work. Always running out to some 'meeting,' but it was never anything with the department." Quincy added air quotes. "I normally wouldn't say all this, but I figured, as his friend, you had a right to know."

I nodded, murmuring my agreement as I processed his words. Had Elijah been acting erratically, or was this man looking for anything to gossip about?

Of course, if I were Elijah's old friend, would I sit quietly while someone made outrageous claims about their dead friend? Elijah hadn't even been gone a week, and already this man was spouting these theories to anyone who would listen. What was he up to?

"I really don't think you should go around spreading rumors like this," I said, leaning forward and narrowing my eyes at him. "Elijah was a good man, and now he's dead. Who knows what killed him, but he sure doesn't need some gossip running around, spouting nonsense."

Quincy leaned back, holding his hands up in surrender. "You're right. I'm so sorry. I'm not saying he did anything to cause this heinous act, just that some of his actions had been strange recently. I did like the man, and I'm sorry he's dead. But I think there may be other things going on here, and, as his friend, I thought you had the right to know."

Quincy paused and glanced down at his hands, smoothing out the skin around his fingers. I leaned my head in slightly to get a closer look. His cuticles were red and raw. Had he been picking at his fingers before I'd shown up? What did he have to be nervous or anxious about? Had the police said something to him when they questioned him about it that caused him to react this way?

"I'm sorry to even suggest that Elijah caused any of this, but it's just my perception of how he'd been acting recently," Quincy said with a sigh. "For all I know, he was in a new relationship and having trouble keeping up with the demands of work. That happens to all of us, doesn't it, when we find someone new?"

Some people did start acting erratically when they entered a new relationship. Was that what had happened here with Elijah?

"A new relationship? Really? Had you met her?"

"No, he never said anything about it. That's just my guess on what might've caused his recent behavior. We didn't talk much about our personal lives. He was always pretty quiet about these kinds of things. Ever since the blow-up with Kristina, I get the sense he kept things pretty close to himself. He didn't want to bring more drama into the college or into his life."

My ears perked up at Kristina's name. I was potentially showing my hand with this next question since an "old friend" of Elijah's should know these things, but I needed to get answers.

"Blow-up with Kristina? What do you mean?"

Quincy cocked his head at me and his mouth turned down in a frown. "His messy divorce? His wife took him to court and tried to take all of his money? I'm surprised you didn't know about this."

His eyes narrowed as he studied me, and I quickly jumped into the pause before he had a chance to wonder why an old friend wouldn't know this.

"Oh right, Kristina," I said with a laugh and a flippant wave of my hand. "How could I forget? But like I said, Elijah and I haven't talked much in recent years. I get updates on Facebook, but I'm not really up-to-date on his life or anything like that. That's what makes all of this so hard to handle. I can't believe I didn't get the chance to see how he's been. He was so young. I wish I knew what happened to him to lead to his death. I wonder if his ex-wife knew anything about why he was acting so erratically."

"I'm not sure," Quincy said with a shake of his head. "She still lives in town. She actually teaches at the college occasionally. I'm not sure what her exact relationship is with the college, but she's become quite a prolific artist in recent years, and she teaches the occasional painting course."

For someone who wasn't very close with Elijah, this man seemed to know a lot about his ex-wife. Were they closer than Quincy was with Elijah? Was there something going on between the two of them that might've led to Elijah's death?

"Did you know Kristina well?"

"Ah, not very well, I'd say. Like I said, she teaches here occasionally and, when they were married, she'd come by the office to meet him for lunch or to drive home together. We'd chat sometimes, but it was all very superficial."

I made a mental note to follow up with Kristina about all this. Would she say the same thing about how well she knew Quincy? Or was Quincy hiding something from me about their relationship?

"I actually think I have her phone number somewhere.

She's been Elijah's emergency contact for years, even after their divorce."

He shuffled through some papers on his desk and pulled out a black notebook, flipping through the pages. He scrawled something down on a slip of paper and passed it my way.

"You might want to try talking to her if you're looking for answers. I know the police are speaking with her soon."

Quincy shifted in his seat again, smoothing out the nonexistent wrinkles on his pants. Even from this far away, I could tell there weren't any wrinkles on those chinos.

"What did you tell the police when they came by? I'm sure they had lots of questions for everyone here."

"Not as many questions as you'd expect, actually, from watching all this on TV," Quincy said, warming up to the topic of the police. "They wanted to know our relationship to Elijah, how long we'd worked with him, that sort of thing. They asked about our alibis as well. They mentioned the attack happened in the morning, two days ago, and they wanted to know where we all were during that time."

Patel had already told me about his time of death, so that wasn't news for me. The big question I now had was: where was this man when Elijah was killed?

"That must've been so scary, getting questioned by the police," I said, crossing my legs. "I bet you'd want to tell them something rock solid, right? Do you think they believed what you told them?"

"They better," Quincy said with a chuckle. "I was teaching an extension class in Seattle on that day. Twenty undergrads and my T.A. can confirm that I was there. Actually, now that you mention it..." Quincy paused and pushed aside the papers on his desk, pulling out a small card from the pile and passing it along to me. "That's the contact info for the detective in Pine Brook who's leading the case. She'll probably want to talk to an old friend of Elijah's."

I smiled tightly and took the card. I had no intention of telling Patel that Elijah's "old friend" was in town, but Quincy didn't need to know that.

I slipped the card into my bag. "I really appreciate you sharing all of this with me. I better get going. I hope they find his killer soon."

We said our goodbyes and I hurried out of his office, keeping my head down as I passed Lisa at the front desk. Hopefully, she'd forget about this visit and not mention it to the police. I didn't want Patel to know I was sticking my nose into her investigation again.

A class must've just let out because the halls of the department were filled with students. I blended in with the crowd and followed the sea of students out into the chilly sun.

10

A s I drove back to the inn, I thought over my conversation with Quincy Martell. He'd been much more forthcoming with information about Elijah than I'd expected. How did he really feel about the man? Was he jealous of the other professor, and therefore trying to overcompensate? Or did he simply love stirring up the department gossip mill and couldn't help himself?

Quincy would have to have been pretty dumb to claim that he'd been teaching in front of students if he hadn't been, so his alibi was probably true. Still, I'd see if I could get any information from the police about where he was when Elijah was killed. Maybe I could convince Lisa at the department to tell me where Quincy was that day.

I still hadn't learned as much as I'd been hoping. I'd wanted to sneak into Elijah's office and snoop around, but Quincy and Lisa had kept me from doing that. Would they leave at some point so I could sneak in? Maybe I'd try again in the evening, before they locked up the building.

I pulled into the inn's parking lot and switched off the engine. Peeking out the window, I groaned. Clouds had moved in on my drive, and the sunny skies had quickly turned into a downpour. I'd be soaked as soon as I left the car.

The inn's dark wood, sloped roof, and lush greenery that climbed up the sides of the building normally brought images of cottages and fairytales to mind when I stood before it, but heavy rain and gloomy skies had a tendency to turn the inn dreary and imposing from the outside. No wonder the winter season was our slowest of the year; images of the eerie inn probably scared off guests.

What was my next step? I wanted to go back to the college and try to snoop around again, but I needed to wait until there were fewer people around. Would Patel confirm Quincy's alibi for me? She hadn't been very helpful in the past when I'd come to her with these questions, believing that a civilian should stay out of police business. And yet, I had helped find a killer. Maybe she'd be more willing to share some information with me.

All I really wanted to do was stay inside the inn for the rest of the day, where it was warm and dry. Sleuthing in the winter season in Washington was much wetter than I expected.

Unfortunately, fate had a different idea for me.

I entered the inn and shook off my raincoat, already feeling my shoulders relax as a fire crackled in the fireplace. While the outside of the Hemlock Inn implied vaulted ceilings and drafty halls, the inside was much cozier than it seemed, with dark wood, the large fireplace, and huge, thick pillows scattered on every surface. All this created the image of curling up with a good book and a hot mug of tea. I began a mental tally of all the books I had on hand, trying to match the subject matter to the mood I was in, when I heard my name.

"You're back! What did you find out?" Chrissy dashed over to my side. She'd been talking with Nadia at the front desk.

I peeked a glance over at Nadia, who was flipping through a magazine, her attention focused on celebrity gossip. The rest of the lobby was empty. I pulled Chrissy over to the fireplace and lowered my voice.

"I wasn't able to get into Elijah's office, but I talked to another professor in the department," I said hurriedly. I told her about Quincy and all the information he'd given me, plus the fact that he had an alibi.

"Wow. I'm surprised he would tell you so much. I actually know Kristina, from back in grad school. Maybe she can tell us more about Elijah."

Before I could say anything else, we were interrupted by Tracy, who'd just entered the lobby.

"There you are," she said, striding over to us. "I was about to call you."

"Everything all right?" I asked.

"I wouldn't take that off so fast." She pointed to my coat. "We've got an appointment in twenty minutes." Tracy pulled her raincoat off the hook and passed mine back to me. "We should get going if we don't want to be late."

"Appointment?" What appointment?

"An appointment to check out some apartments. I mentioned it earlier this week, remember? We've got two to see today."

I smacked my hand against my head as realization dawned. Drat. Tracy had mentioned wanting to start looking for a new apartment for me to move into, so we could start offering the suite I was staying in to guests. Since finding Elijah's body, I'd forgotten all about it.

"Shouldn't someone stay here to keep an eye on things?"

I asked, gesturing around the lobby. Even as I said it, I knew the excuse was weak. The lobby was empty, and Nadia yawned at the front desk as she flipped the pages of her magazine.

I wasn't in the mood to go back out into the rain and commit to a year lease on a place that probably hadn't been upgraded since the '70s. I'd seen enough of Pine Brook to know what I was likely to find on the apartment market, and I wasn't eager to face my options. Besides, I liked living at the inn. It helped me to feel closer to Aunt Sylvia.

"Don't worry, Nadia can take care of things here. We'll be able to bring in a lot of extra money if we can get you out of that suite."

Was that the real reason Tracy wanted me to find a new apartment, or did she want me out of Sylvia's former suite for some other reason? Was this her first step in driving me out of the inn altogether? I was being ridiculous, but I couldn't help the anxious thoughts from fluttering around my head.

"I shouldn't leave Chrissy," I said, quickly finding some new excuse to throw Tracy's way.

"I'll be fine," Chrissy piped up. "I'd join you, but I really don't want to go out into the rain. I'll see if I can find the phone number of that person we were talking about," she added with a wink.

With that, she scurried out of the lobby, pulling out her cell phone. I narrowed my eyes at her departure. Was she about to find Kristina and grill her about her ex-husband? Or would she do the smart thing and wait for me to come back so we could figure out what to do together?

"All right," I said with a sigh, my excuses down the drain. "Let's go check out those apartments."

"Great." Tracy grinned widely.

At that moment, a crash of thunder sounded from outside, and the rain picked up speed.

"I'm sure it'll be fine," Tracy said, steering me out of the inn. "We can handle a little rain."

BY THE TIME we showed up to the first apartment, my jeans were soaked through, and dark clouds had rolled in. Tracy promised we would be quick, and we ducked into the lobby of the apartment building.

She'd driven, and she'd explained about these places on the drive over.

"This first one is a studio unit in a building only five minutes away from the inn by car. How can you beat that commute?"

The inn always felt remote when you were in it, but after a short drive you were launched right back into town and civilization. This apartment was one of the first buildings on the drive from the inn and would keep my commute short. Its rent was cheap, dirt cheap compared to what I'd been paying in L.A., and cheap enough that I wouldn't mind forking it over every month. The inn paid me a salary out of its coffers, but it wasn't much, and I'd been able to save some up some money while staying in the suite onsite.

The money we'd earn by renting out the suite to guests wouldn't come back to me directly, but it would allow us to make some necessary repairs around the inn and not feel like we were scrimping. At least, not too much scrimping; any small business had a certain amount of scrimping.

Once parked in front of the building, we slid into our raincoats and ran into the lobby, though we were still soaked by the time we got inside. The lobby was quiet, with a row of mailboxes along the far wall and several potted plants adorning the space. I sniffed Lysol in the air, like someone had recently scrubbed down the surfaces, but it couldn't quite hide the scent of cigarette smoke. I smirked at the *No Smoking* sign by the mailboxes.

The building was three stories tall and spread out long, so we trudged up the stairs to the second floor. Tracy knocked on one of the units and we were welcomed in by the landlord.

Coming from L.A. and living on a meager bartender's salary, I'd seen some bad apartments. Cockroaches, leaking faucets, loud neighbors who smoked cigarettes on the patio above yours so the smoke drifted down and permeated your curtains. This place made me miss those cockroaches.

It was a studio, not much larger than my suite at the inn, but with much less charm. A bare lightbulb hung from the ceiling and offered hardly any illumination in the room. One window let in very little light, especially with the gray clouds outside. Given that it was now officially winter, it would probably be this dark most of the time. A kitchenette was in the corner, with a hotplate as the only source of heat for food.

A toilet sat in the middle of the room, with a curtain wrapped around it for "privacy." I stopped in my tracks at the site of the "bathroom." How in the world would you have a house party with the amenities smack dab in the middle of the room? No scenario I could come up with seemed ideal.

Next to the kitchenette was the shower, which was just a shower-head and some tile, with another flimsy curtain wrapped around it. A full-sized bed was pushed up against the wall, and it was clear a bigger bed wouldn't fit in the space. One curtain hung against the wall and, when I poked my head behind it, I saw a clothing rack that was apparently masquerading as a closet.

"Do you allow pets?" I asked the landlord, struggling for any question that would redeem this place in my eyes.

Lola couldn't stay onsite at the inn without someone there watching her, so she was going to be my new room-mate. Tracy would've happily taken the dog, but she lived with a cat who wasn't interested in another roommate.

The landlord shook his head and opened his mouth to say something—to try to convince me that this place just needed a little "sprucing up"?—but I grabbed Tracy's arm and dragged her out of the apartment before he could say anything. I shouted thanks over my shoulder and stomped Tracy down the stairs. No way was I going anywhere without Lola.

"Okay, so now we know what we don't like," Tracy said as we buckled into her car, her voice cheery even as thunder clapped in the distance.

No amount of smiles and positive thinking could improve that place or the rainstorm we were now officially stuck in.

I groaned and pressed my head back against the head-rest. "Please tell me this next place is better."

It wasn't.

Though bigger, and with an actual closet, we could hear the neighbors stomping around in their rooms above us as we stood in the living room. This place had an actual kitchen, though the appliances looked like they were from the fifties, and the tile throughout the apartment had me concerned about Lola slipping and sliding as she walked around.

There were more windows and a fire escape that the landlord explained was nice to sit on when the weather was good, but the unit faced the highway and all I could hear were trucks whooshing by. This place was also three times the rent of the previous unit and not much cheaper than my apartment in L.A. Given the lack of sun in Pine Brook—meaning I wouldn't get much use out of the fire escape until the summer—I wasn't thrilled about paying so much more for a worse place.

"I'm sorry it's not quite what you're looking for," Tracy said as we looked around. "It's been a while since I've shopped for apartments. The options are...different, to say the least."

"Are you sure I need to leave the inn right now? Can't I stay for a little while longer until we find someplace better?" I hated asking, as I knew the smart thing to do was to open up the suite to paying guests, but if these two places were any indication of the kinds of apartments I was going to find in Pine Brook, then I was getting desperate.

Tracy grimaced. "You know we need to do this."

"Not your flavor?" the landlord asked when she realized we weren't interested in the place.

I didn't know what my "flavor" was, but I shook my head. "It's still early in my search. I'm trying to figure out exactly what I'm looking for."

"Well, I show a bunch of listings around town and in Holliston," she said, passing me her card. "Check out my website online and see if anything piques your interest. I'd be happy to do another showing somewhere else in town."

"Thanks." I glanced at the card before slipping it into my pocket. I hadn't realized she was a realtor and not a landlord.

"We should probably get back to the Hemlock," Tracy said to me as the three of us walked towards the front door.

"I don't want to keep us away too long. I'm sure we'll find someplace great for you."

"Oh, you work at the Hemlock Inn?" the realtor asked as we stood in the entryway and slipped on our coats. Her card had identified her as Vivian Pierce.

I nodded, adjusting my coat and zipping up the zipper. "We run it."

"Great to meet you both," Vivian said with a smile. She was in her fifties, with sleek blonde hair cut in a bob and long, gleaming red fingernails that clacked against any surface she touched.

"Like I said, I show a bunch of different listings in the area, so I'm happy to help you find the right place. Did I hear that you were the one who found that body behind Cheesy Does It?"

I grimaced and nodded. I'd already gotten caught up in one murder investigation and still dealt with funny looks from people at the grocery store. I wasn't interested in being associated with another death.

"Such a shame," Vivian said with a shake of her head. "I've lived in Pine Brook my whole life, and I've never seen anything like it. With those deaths last month, too, clearly something's going on in Pine Brook. It's not safe out there anymore. This whole country is going to hell in a hand-basket."

I wasn't interested in getting into a discussion with this woman about the state of our country or of our town, and a glance at Tracy told me she agreed, so I smiled and nodded.

"Yes, well, Elijah was from Holliston, so the killer is probably from there. Pine Brook has had some bad luck recently, but I'm sure there's nothing to be worried about."

Vivian nodded. "You're probably right. Still, you can't be too careful."

"It does make me wonder, though," I said, glancing at Tracy and back to Vivian, and wondering why I didn't drop this. It was like my mind couldn't stop thinking about Elijah's death and what had happened. "He was from Holliston—that's where he taught and lived—so why was he in Pine Brook? That still confuses me. I don't get the sense that many people from Holliston spend much time in Pine Brook."

"Oh, I know why," Vivian said, and my eyebrows shot up my face at her words.

"Or at least I can guess," she continued. "He was looking for an apartment. He found me online and sent me an email, asking if I had any places in Pine Brook on the market. We talked on the phone and I told him about this place, but it wasn't exactly what he was looking for. He was renting a house in Holliston, but it was too small. He said he needed a second bedroom for his musical instruments. I guess he played the guitar and the viola."

I barely heard her talk about Elijah's musical talents as the impact of her words came over me. Elijah was trying to move to Pine Brook? Why? Was that why he was in town the day he'd been killed? Brunch with friends, then apartment shopping?

"Did he say why he was looking in Pine Brook?" I asked. "I'd assume he'd have a nice place in Holliston since he'd been at the college for so many years."

"That's what I thought, too," Vivian said, "and that's what I asked him. But he said he was dealing with a stalker and wanted to leave Holliston as soon as his lease was up. He couldn't go too far since he was still teaching, but he hoped Pine Brook would be safer." A gleam in Vivian's eyes had me wondering how much she was enjoying sharing this gossip about a dead man.

"He said he had a stalker?" Tracy asked, her voice incredulous, and I had to agree with her implication.

It seemed strange that Elijah would admit something so personal to a realtor he'd just met, and Vivian had the good grace to acknowledge her exaggeration.

"He didn't say *stalker*, exactly, but he said a student had figured out where his house was in Holliston and kept popping by. But I could tell there was more going on with this man. He looked so... despondent, like if he couldn't get out of Holliston, he wasn't sure what was going to happen."

"Did he know which student? Had he gone to the police about it?" This information was very relevant to the murder investigation. Was Patel already aware of this stalker?

"I'm sorry, I don't know anything else," Vivian said. "I probably shouldn't even have mentioned this. I hope the police find his killer soon."

Tracy and I thanked Vivian for her time and shuffled out of the apartment. As we ran through the rain back to Tracy's car, my mind was spinning with the implications of what Vivian had told us. It seemed like everyone in this town knew some piece of gossip about someone else and were only too eager to share it if the right person came asking. I'd experienced this last month when dealing with another murder investigation, and it was all happening again.

What was Elijah trying to escape in Holliston? Why did he decide to come to Pine Brook? Tacoma was not that far from Holliston, and a much bigger city, and Elijah would've had an easier chance of hiding out from this stalker there. What about Pine Brook had been more appealing to him?

Who was this student Vivian had mentioned? Had one of his students fallen in love with him and murdered him when he didn't return their feelings?

My mind spun with the possibilities, and I stared out the window at the rain, trying to put the pieces together.

As Tracy drove us back to the inn, I realized I needed to talk to Patel. I was upset at her for questioning my sister's innocence, but she was the lead detective on this case, and I'd stumbled onto something important. Plus, a student stalker would only strengthen Chrissy's innocence.

11

"I know those two weren't ideal," Tracy said, pulling into the inn's parking lot.

I snorted at her use of the word "ideal."

She smirked. "Okay, they were as far from ideal as you could get. But we'll find someplace you'll love. It's tougher to find a place for a single person, but it's not impossible. I know we can do it."

"I promise to keep an open mind about this," I said with a smile, ignoring the sting at "single person."

I'd looked at enough postings online to understand that most of the homes for sale or rent in the area were for large families looking to settle down. All the apartments were garbage because all the "single people" in town didn't have much choice. Somehow, Tracy had managed to scoop up a good place. Would there be anything left for me?

Maybe this meant I needed to branch out into Holliston. Adding thirty minutes to my commute every day wasn't at the top of my list of things I wanted to do, but it was the right decision for the inn. We could bring in a lot of money if we opened up the suite, and I knew Tracy had big plans for the place. I didn't want to get in the way of that.

Tracy and I dashed into the building, shaking off the rain from our raincoats as we stood in the lobby. Chrissy was reading a book in front of the fireplace, and she hopped up as we entered.

"How'd it go?" she asked.

"It's a work in progress," Tracy said, striding over to the front desk.

"Apartment shopping is never easy, right?" I said to Chrissy, joining her in front of the fire. "But we'll keep looking."

"Well, good luck," Chrissy said. "I know how tough it is in L.A. I hope it's not as bad here."

Some could argue that it was worse here, in certain ways, but I didn't want to get into it.

"We did learn something interesting about Elijah," I said, lowering my voice and leaning in closer. I quickly told her about the realtor and that Elijah was looking for a new place in Pine Brook because of a stalker.

"Really?" Her voice was incredulous. "A stalker?"

I shrugged. "That's what Vivian told us." I glanced at my watch. "I actually shouldn't stay—I want to tell Detective Patel what I learned. You should probably stay here. The police don't need to know that you're involved in any of this."

Chrissy nodded. "You're right. Just be careful, okay?"

"I will."

I left her in the lobby, grabbing my coat and dashing back out into the rain. I dialed Patel's number as I slid behind the wheel. Her greeting was curt.

"I have some information about Elijah Norris' death." I didn't wait for her response before pointing my car in the direction of the police station. "Meet at the station in fifteen minutes?"

She grunted. "You're lucky you caught me at my desk. See you soon." She hung up without saying goodbye.

Detective Patel and I had had several run-ins last month after I'd stumbled onto a dead body and decided to play Jessica Fletcher. We weren't friends, as she'd threatened to arrest me on multiple occasions, but I'd like to think I'd earned her respect and trust. At the very least, she was willing to hear me out when I said I had information to share.

The Pine Brook Police Department wasn't very big, since the town itself wasn't very big, and Patel was one of only a few other detectives. I'd met a few of the patrol officers, like Officer Scott, and tended to steer clear of the chief of police, Tate, who hated me from the moment he met me. Granted, I'd been butting my nose into his murder investigation when we met, but you'd think he'd be more appreciative of the help. I could understand it, though—I didn't like it when people tried to tell me how to run the inn.

Still, as I pulled into the parking lot of the station, I sent up a short prayer that I wouldn't run into Tate. He'd yelled at me enough times in the past month that I'd resorted to avoiding him whenever I saw him at the grocery store. He might've taken issue with the fact that I was now involved in another one of his cases.

The police station was as drab as ever in the rain, with a bullpen of open offices and cubicles inside, and assorted conference and interview rooms branching off the center. Patel met me at the front lobby of the station and led me back to one of the small rooms. It wasn't an interrogation room, at least not like the ones on TV. This looked more like a conference room.

She sat me down at the table and took a seat across from me, pulling out her notepad. "Talk."

"I met a realtor earlier today." I dug Vivian's card out of my bag and passed it across the table. "I'm looking for a new apartment, and she said Elijah Norris had been apartment hunting in Pine Brook. Vivian thought Elijah had a stalker —he told her that one of his students had found his house in Holliston and wouldn't leave him alone."

Patel studied Vivian's card, then made a note on her notepad. "Did you tell this Ms. Pierce to come to the station to make a statement?"

"No. I didn't think about that."

Patel scribbled something on her notepad, then leaned back in her seat. "This is why you're not a police officer. You don't know the rules. I can't take your claim about a stalker as fact without confirming it with Ms. Pierce. Otherwise, it's just hearsay."

"Well, all right, then go talk to her." I gestured to the card. "Her number's right on there, and she seemed eager to share what she'd learned with me."

Patel slipped Vivian's card into her notepad, then shut it. Guess I wasn't getting Vivian's card back.

"Why were you talking to this woman about Elijah Norris? What happened to lying low and staying out of things?"

I held up my hands in a placating gesture. "I promise this wasn't me sleuthing or anything." I held back the fact that I'd been to Holliston College to talk to Quincy. "Like I said, I'm apartment hunting, and when I mentioned owning the Hemlock, Vivian knew that I'd been at Cheesy Does It when Elijah was found. She remembered the murders last month and has some...opinions about the crime rate in Pine Brook."

Patel rolled her eyes. "Everyone in this town has opinions about our crime rate. In fact, when you run the numbers, crime has been down over the past fifteen years, but all anyone wants to talk about is their best friend's mother's plumber who was mugged downtown."

This town had already had three murders in the short time I'd been in town, so it wasn't like crime was nonexistent. But Patel clearly had feelings about this topic, so I kept my opinions to myself.

"I appreciate you bringing me this information, but you need to keep your nose out of this, okay?" Patel's voice was stern. "We're dealing with a killer; I can't let a civilian get involved."

"I understand. I just want to keep my sister safe. But I'll stay out of things." I didn't want to get face-to-face with a killer again, so staying out of things was probably a good idea.

Suddenly, the room's door burst open. Chief Tate was on the other side, his face red and suspicious.

"What are you doing here?" he snarled, gesturing to me.

"Sir, she's here to report on information about the Norris case," Patel said, standing. I followed suit.

"Oh really? Detective, why would you need the help of a civilian on your murder case?" He turned his beady eyes onto Patel, his voice dripping with sarcasm.

"I was trying to help." I couldn't let Patel take the blame for this on her own. "I figured you'd want me to bring information that might help you find a killer."

Tate turned his gaze back to me, his eyes narrow. "Listen, missy, we don't need your help around here. You've already stuck your nose in where it doesn't belong once. If I see you messing around with one of my cases again, I'll have you arrested. Now leave."

I scurried out of the room, glancing over at Patel as I left. Her face said she wished she'd never brought me back here in the first place. I skirted around Tate and left.

Tate was a bully, and I'd had to hold my tongue not to go off on him. Someone truly interested in finding killers and bringing about justice would take help however they could get it. However, Tate didn't like what he couldn't control, and I'd already proven that I didn't care what he thought. As long as I could keep sharing information with Patel, I'd let Tate stomp around like a toddler with a tantrum for as long as he'd like.

12

After dealing with Tate's outburst and sharing Vivian Pierce's information about Elijah's stalker with Patel, I came back to the inn prepared to let the police run their investigation while I stayed out of things. I still wanted the chance to snoop around Elijah's office, but I didn't want to do anything that would cause Tate to turn his anger more directly to my sister. He could be vindictive when he wanted to, as I'd already learned last month in a different case.

Imagine my surprise when, the next morning at breakfast, Chrissy's phone rang with a call from Kristina, Elijah's ex-wife.

"What a lovely surprise." Chrissy shot me a glance, her eyes wide. Why was Elijah's ex-wife calling Chrissy?

"I'm so sorry about Elijah," Chrissy said into the phone, turning her body away from me as if to keep me from snooping. Fat chance of that! "I wanted to reach out and see how you were doing, but I didn't know if you were still in town...What's that?... Oh yes, I'm staying in Pine Brook with my sister. She owns an inn here.... Oh, I'm not really sure. A couple more days, maybe?" She paused and listened to Kristina speak on the other end, and I strained to catch a hint of anything. I knew she wouldn't put the call on speakerphone while we were sitting in public, but still, I wanted to know what was going on.

"That's really sweet of you," Chrissy said, the color draining from her face. "Text me the address and time. Looking forward to seeing you." She said her goodbyes and hung up, keeping her gaze down and sipping her coffee.

"What was that about?" I asked after a few moments of silence. If she wasn't going to offer anything up, then I was going to have to yank it out of her.

Chrissy sighed. "That was Elijah's ex-wife, Kristina. They started dating after Elijah and I broke up. I haven't seen her in years. She heard I was in town and somehow got my number."

"What was that about inviting you someplace? Does she want to talk about Elijah?"

Maybe Kristina had some clue about what had happened to Elijah and wanted to share it with my sister. I could feel my investigative senses tingling, even as I reminded myself that I was supposed to stay out of this murder case. If the clues came to me, I couldn't really do anything about that, right?

Chrissy shook her head. "No. She invited us to Elijah's funeral."

Two days later, Chrissy and I stood outside the Holliston Community Church, dressed in the finest black dresses we could find with two days' notice. I tugged at the hem of my dress and glanced around, teetering on the heels Chrissy had lent me when I'd shown her the only shoes I had were running shoes and winter boots. She always packed an extra set of heels when she traveled, and, fortunately, we'd been the same size shoe since high school. Unfortunately for me, she liked them tall.

We'd spent the time in between keeping quiet at the inn, both of us wondering if the police were gathering more evidence against Chrissy. I wanted to know if Patel had learned anything about Elijah's stalker, but thought it best not to make any more trouble for her with Tate. The police had finished up their tests on Chrissy's rental car, but they wouldn't tell us if they'd found anything.

Chrissy had finally called Mark and told him what was going on, though she didn't mention that she'd been brought to the police station. She worried that, if he knew, he'd race up here in a heartbeat, and she didn't want to scare Hannah. I just hoped I wouldn't have to call him in a week and tell him his wife had been officially arrested for murder.

I glanced around the front of the church, where guests were milling before the doors opened for the services. Where was Kristina? Would I recognize her in the crowd? After spending my evening a few nights ago stalking her online presence, I figured that would be the last I'd hear of her unless she had, of course, killed her husband.

As the pastor opened the doors and welcomed everyone into the church, I glanced over at Chrissy. She'd been silent on the drive over to Holliston. Well, really, she'd been silent ever since that call with Kristina. She hadn't told me anything else Kristina had said, just that she wanted to see Chrissy and hoped she could pay her respects. And, of course, as her sister, I was invited as well.

We filed into the church and took our seats in the pews. The last time I'd been in a church had been in college, when I'd studied abroad in Italy. That country was bursting with churches, and I'd spent a lot of time touring them. This church was smaller and less ornate than those had been, but looked well used. Dark wood, arched beams, images of Jesus throughout the space, and gray carpeting muffled our footsteps and chatter.

I'd been surprised to learn that the funeral was happening so soon after Elijah's murder. Typically, I'd expect the police to need time with the body to solve the crime. Maybe Elijah's ex-wife had convinced them to let her have the body sooner for some reason.

Once everyone was seated, the doors of the church were opened again, and a woman walked through them, led by a man on her arm. She was glamorous, and easily outshined the man standing next to her, even though he was tall and striking himself. I realized with a start that this was Kristina.

Her hair had grown out a bit from her photos on Facebook, though it still barely reached her shoulders in a shaggy bob. Her cheekbones were even more striking in person, and dark sunglasses shielded her eyes. She was tall and thin, though her posture managed to make her look modelesque, rather than gaunt. She was wearing a slip of a dress with six-inch heels that looked like she'd been born in those shoes.

She drifted past us, leaving behind the scent of lavender and rose water in her wake. The man led her to a pew in the front and settled her into her seat. Once she was seated, the services began.

MY BACK ITCHED in a place I couldn't reach. Chrissy's heels were beginning to pinch my toes, and the black dress that Tracy had loaned me was made from a fabric that did not pair well with my skin. The pastor at the front of the church had been going on for the last—quick glance at my watch—

forty minutes, and didn't look ready to stop. I didn't recognize anyone sitting in the crowd, which made sense. This was Holliston, and these were probably all fellow professors or people Elijah had known back in grad school, like Chrissy. I'd only been in Pine Brook for a few short weeks and had barely left the town.

Wait a minute. My gaze was caught on the gray head of someone bobbing in the back row. I strained my eyes and leaned out into the aisle for a closer look, ignoring the glare from the woman sitting behind me. Was that...? My mouth dropped open in shock. What was Estelle doing here?

She was in the back of the church, her head down but definitely sneaking around. I glanced back up to the front of the church, but the pastor was still talking, something about the eternity of life and death and the lifespan of butterflies, or something like that—I wasn't really paying attention— and everyone in the crowd had their gaze on him. I glanced back at Estelle in the back row and saw her sneak off into a side room.

"Just need to run to the bathroom," I whispered to Chrissy, who was focused on the pastor and barely registered that I was leaving.

I left my purse on my seat and slipped out of the pew, grateful that the carpeted floors muffled the sounds of my heels. I hurried down the aisle and popped into the room Estelle had snuck into.

"What are you doing?" I hissed after shutting the door softly behind me.

Estelle jumped and turned around in surprise, holding a vase she'd picked up from one of the tables in the room.

"Simone, how lovely to see you," she said, trying to hold the vase behind her back but failing miserably.

I hurried over to her and snatched the vase out of her

hand, settling it back in its place. "Don't play coy with me. As soon as I saw your little head sneaking around, I knew something was up. What are you doing here?"

"Same as you. I heard about the funeral and wanted to find the killer."

We kept our voices low, listening to see if anyone approached the room from the outside.

I groaned and smacked my palm against my head. Of course she came here looking for the killer. "And you think the killer is here? Did you see anything?"

Estelle shrugged. "It only makes sense. Of course the killer would want to show up to the funeral. He'd want to make sure his victim was really dead."

"How do you know the killer hasn't fled town? Why would he show up and risk getting caught?"

Shuffling came from the next room over. The services must have been ending.

"Look, we need to get out of here, now, before someone sees us." I grabbed her arm and dragged her out of the room, ignoring her protests.

Back in the main room of the church, the service had ended and people had started standing up. Kristina moved to the front of the church, and people began to line up to pay their respects to her. Chrissy had left the pew and made her way to the line. I was not interested in staying any longer while I had a funeral crasher to deal with.

"There you are," Chrissy said when we came over to her. She passed me my purse. "I worried you'd left already. What's she doing here?" she asked, glancing at Estelle.

"Come to pay my respects, of course," Estelle said before I had a chance to say anything. "Life is so precious. I like to keep an eye on the funerals around here. Some people don't have anyone show up to their funeral, and I'd hate for any family to feel like their dead relative didn't have any friends."

I stared at her, my eyebrows raised. As far as lies go, it wasn't half-bad. It made her seem like a kook, but it wasn't too unbelievable.

"I think we should probably go," I said.

Chrissy shook her head. "I want to see Kristina."

The receiving line moved fast—what is there to say to an ex-wife?—so Chrissy was in front of Kristina in a matter of minutes.

The tall widow pulled my sister into a hug. "Chrissy, I'm so glad you could make it."

"Thank you so much for the invitation," Chrissy said, pulling away from Kristina. "I'm sorry for not reaching out sooner."

"Don't even worry about it, darling," Kristina said, and it did look like she genuinely didn't mind it. "I'm happy to see you again, even if it is under these circumstances. I thought you were down in Los Angeles? What brings you up to Washington?"

"My sister," Chrissy said, gesturing over to me. I smiled and gave a tiny wave as Kristina turned her piercing gaze onto me. "She runs an inn in Pine Brook, and I had come up for a visit, when we...learned about his death."

"Are you the ones who found him? I'd heard it was the owner of the Hemlock Inn, but I didn't realize you were there too, Chrissy. Somehow, it makes me feel better to hear that a friend was there with him, and not just a bunch of strangers. But what a dreadful way for you both to meet Elijah," she added, turning to Estelle and me.

"And I'm Estelle," Estelle said, butting her way past me and holding out her hand. "My condolences, dear. I've heard such good things about your husband. He was taken too soon."

"Oh, you are kind," Kristina said, shaking her hand. "He was technically my ex-husband, though I did love him up until the day he died. Why don't we head outside together?"

She gestured to the pastor, who began to lead people out of the church. Kristina slipped her arm through Chrissy's and led her through a different door, and Estelle and I followed.

Outside, the air was chilly, but the sun had come out. Kristina led us down a path that overlooked the cemetery. Other guests headed down the main road to the cemetery, and they looked like little ants as they walked. Up ahead, the path we were on would lead us to them eventually, but for the most part, we were alone. Maybe now was my chance to ask Kristina some questions and find out more about her ex-husband.

"I am so sorry about Elijah," I told her.

"Thank you," Kristina said. "It's so hard to believe he's gone. I thought we'd have more time together, you know? Though our marriage was over, our friendship never was. We were still close."

"I still can't believe it," Chrissy said as we headed down the path. "Elijah was so full of life. The world seems smaller with him gone."

With an exclamation of surprise, Chrissy suddenly teetered to the side, almost falling to the ground. Kristina, Estelle, and I quickly hurried to her side, grabbing her arms before she had a chance to fall.

"Are you all right?" I asked, holding her steady and glancing around to see what had happened.

"Yes, I'm fine," she said. "My heel broke!"

Her ankle turned, exposing the broken shoe. It must've gotten caught on a rock on the path we were walking down.

Estelle gripped Chrissy's arm, propping her up against her. "Why don't we head inside and see if we can fix this?" she asked Chrissy. "These two can keep walking down. We don't want to get in the way of the funeral."

Chrissy agreed, and the two women began to shuffle back up the path to the church. Kristina turned to head back down towards the cemetery, and I caught Estelle's eye before turning around. She motioned towards Kristina, nodding her head enthusiastically, and I realized she wanted me to question Kristina while I had her alone. I ignored the voice in my head that reminded me about what I had promised Patel and followed after Kristina.

"Tell me more about Elijah," I said, linking my arm through hers to keep us both steady as we walked down the dirt path.

"He was a great man. So intelligent and kind. Our marriage had its issues, of course, but we never stopped loving each other." Her smile was dreamy and nostalgic.

"I can't even imagine what you're going through right now. When was the last time you saw him?" I asked.

"Just a week ago, actually. Truth be told, we were reconciling. We'd stayed friends after the divorce, but we were finally getting to the point where I thought maybe we'd get back together. We'd been talking on the phone in the weeks leading up to his death, working through our problems and trying to figure out if we wanted to get back together. It's what makes all of this so hard to believe. Things were finally looking good again."

Tears began rolling down her face, and I paused to give her a moment to herself. It was always hard to talk to widows, and I felt my heart break a little at such raw emotion. She slipped a handkerchief out from her pocket and wiped her eyes. I patted her arm soothingly.

While she smoothed away the tears, I thought about what she'd said about her and Elijah reconciling. Their recent Facebook posts hadn't made it seem like they were getting back together, but people didn't put everything on Facebook. Plus, if they were talking on the phone about their relationship, that wouldn't show up on Facebook. Besides, she really did look upset at Elijah's death.

"It must be so difficult to know that someone did this to him," I said gently. "It's already hard enough to lose someone you care about, but to have them taken from you? That's the worst. Have the police spoken to you about it?"

She nodded. "Earlier this week. I imagine they're talking to everyone in Elijah's life. I was the only family he had left —his parents passed away a few years ago, and he didn't have any siblings. All he had was his work."

"Did the police say anything about what they thought happened to him? Chrissy and I found him, of course, but we left as soon as we could, so I don't know much about what led to his death. Do they have a suspect in mind?"

"I'm not sure. They weren't very forthcoming with me. The detective, a woman, she seemed pretty closed off about everything. She did ask for my alibi, which I suppose I should expect as his ex-wife." She gave a little laugh at that.

I paused, holding my breath, hoping she would fill the silence on her own without me having to ask.

"Apparently, he was killed in the late morning," she went on. I let out the breath I was holding. "Fortunately for me, I was in a car going across the Tacoma Narrows Bridge to Gig Harbor at the time. I was driving to see an art studio out there that I'm considering for a partnership. I had to cross a toll bridge and everything, so I'm sure there's proof I was nowhere near the crime scene."

Electronic and photographic evidence of your car crossing a bridge at the same time your ex is killed? Not bad for an alibi. Question was, was it true? The police could pull toll records and likely already had the answer. Could I convince Patel to tell me what she'd learned?

"I hope I'm not overstepping here," I said once Kristina looked ready to talk again. "But I can't stop thinking about who might've wanted to kill your husband. Can you think of anyone who might've done this?"

"I'm not sure," Kristina said, her voice still shaky. "I already spoke with the police and told them I didn't know much. There is one thing, though—I think someone was following Elijah around. He thought one of his students was more interested in him than she should've been. She kept showing up at his house. He was pretty freaked out by it. He wouldn't tell me who it was. I told him to go to the police, but he didn't think she was really a threat."

"You're sure it was a woman?" This matched with what Vivian had already told me about the stalker. Who was this student following Elijah around?

Kristina nodded. "Yes. I guess a lot of the girls who took his classes developed feelings for him. Can you blame them? He was quite a catch."

We'd wound our way down the path and were now at the gravesite with the rest of the guests. Flowers were dispersed all around and the sun was beaming down on us all. Chrissy and Estelle had fixed Chrissy's shoe and had made their way down to the gravesite with the rest of the mourners. The four of us stood in a group, watching everyone arrive.

"Kristina, my dear, there you are." Quincy, the professor

from Elijah's college, stepped forward. His gaze landed on me, and his eyes quirked with a question. "Samantha, I didn't realize you were coming to the funeral."

Three heads swiveled my way as Kristina, Estelle, and Chrissy looked at me in confusion. How was I going to explain this one?

13

"I thought you said your name was Simone?" Kristina turned her gaze on me as Quincy joined us.

"Of course," I said with a laugh, holding my hand out to Quincy. "You must've misunderstood before. My name is Simone, and this is my sister Chrissy, and this here is Estelle. Great to see you again."

Quincy shook our hands on autopilot, his eyes narrowed. He clearly didn't understand why I had lied to him about my name when we first met, or why I was lying now, but he didn't seem likely to call me out on it. He'd seen us talking with Kristina and probably wasn't sure if she'd believe him if he accused me of lying. I couldn't tell how close the two of them were, but people weren't likely in general to call out a liar if they thought the tables could be turned on them.

"Quincy, thank you so much for coming." Kristina held out her hands to the man, and the two of them embraced.

Estelle studied Quincy and Kristina, while Chrissy quirked her brow at me. Though I'd told her about talking to Quincy, I hadn't mentioned the lie. Was she impressed by my quick thinking, or wondering how her baby sister managed to get herself into all these wacky situations?

The pastor marched up to the gravesite and called for quiet over the crowd. He led us through a prayer as dirt was shoveled over Elijah's grave. The man Kristina had entered the church with came over and stood by her side. Was this family?

The pastor finished his prayers and announced that cookies and coffee were being set out back in the church. The crowd began dispersing, and I glanced around, wondering if Elijah's killer was among us. Were they secretly pleased with the events of today?

"Thanks for your support," Kristina said to the man she'd entered the church with. "I'm going to talk to these people for a little bit, but I'll find you later."

The man shot us all a smile, then walked over to another group of mourners.

"My cousin," Kristina explained after he'd left. "He flew in when he heard about Elijah's death."

"Tell me," Estelle said before Quincy had a chance to leave us. I knew she was eager for the opportunity to question a suspect. "How did you know Elijah again?"

"We were in the same department," Quincy explained. "We worked together for years. Such a shame what's happened to him. All the students loved him so much. Now the department needs to figure out how to reallocate his classes. We only have so many professors in our department, and many of us are going to have to pick up the slack left by him. Not that I'm blaming him, of course," he added hurriedly. "He can't be to blame when someone else kills him. I just wish he was more responsible about things." He sniffed, wiping a speck of dirt off his sleeve.

"Yes, I think we all agree that we wish he hadn't been

killed," Kristina said, her tone indicating that she thought Quincy was an idiot. Who calls someone out for being irresponsible at their funeral?

"There seem to be a lot of people here," I said. "I think you're right about Elijah being popular with the students. I wonder if the police have questioned some of these people."

"I didn't know many of the people Elijah worked with." Kristina looked around the gathering. "Like I said, we'd been divorced for years. I still sometimes teach at the college, but it's in a different department. I mostly only know Quincy these days."

"Why are you so interested in the people here?" Quincy's gaze was steady on me. "I'd imagine we should leave the investigating to the police."

Estelle piped up from next to me. "I liken myself to an amateur detective. I try to come to funerals to make sure the deceased aren't buried alone, but once I realized this was Elijah Norris' funeral, I decided to do a little poking around. Don't tell the cops," she added with a wink.

Kristina shot a look at me, her eyes questioning. I only smiled. I'd been honest with Kristina about my intentions to try to find her ex-husband's killer, but Quincy didn't need to know that. I'd let him think Estelle was telling the whole truth.

"Speaking of his murder," Estelle said. Was that what we were speaking of? "I know this is a little crass, but how were you able to get Elijah's body back from the police so soon?" She turned her question to Kristina.

The woman grinned sheepishly. "There's no body in that coffin." She gestured up to the gravesite. "The police said they were holding onto his body pending further tests related to the initial autopsy. God, I can't believe I'm even saying something like that." She gave a shake of her head, her eyes sparkling with tears. She took a couple deep breaths, then continued. "I knew everyone at the college was grieving. I figured if we could hold the ceremony and give everyone a chance to say their goodbyes, it might help with the grieving process."

We nodded and murmured our agreement, though we all had to be thinking the same thing—what kind of wacko holds a funeral without a body? True, grieving happened differently for everyone, and maybe this funeral was also a chance for Kristina to work through her feelings about her ex. The behavior was odd, though. Kristina was staying on my suspect list, no matter how kind and upset she seemed to be.

"It's so hard to say who might've killed Elijah." Quincy smoothed out his suit jacket as he looked around the cemetery. Still no wrinkles on his clothes, though he couldn't seem to stop smoothing them out. "Like I said, everyone loved him, including myself. Well, loved *working* with him, of course. We were all professional. But he was great at his job. It's a shame he's gone." He smoothed out his tie and cleared his throat.

Quincy kept saying the same thing over and over about Elijah, that it was a shame that he was dead. Was he simply repeating a phrase he'd taught himself to appear normal, when really he was glad Elijah was gone? Did he actually hate working with Elijah and killed him because he was getting in the way of something he wanted? A better position at the college, perhaps?

This motive was weak, as lots of people harbor ill-will towards their colleagues but don't kill them, and his alibi was easily proven, giving him less reason to lie about it. Still, I had to wonder if his words hid a deeper malice.

"Well, it's been lovely seeing you all," Quincy said,

glancing down at his watch. "But I should get going. I've got an appointment back at the college." He turned to Kristina and gripped her hand. "Please let me know if I can do anything to help during this time. We're all thinking about you and keeping you and Elijah in our thoughts."

He turned to Chrissy, Estelle, and me. "You three stay safe," he added with a little wave, then left the cemetery. Quincy filed out with the last remaining guests, making us the only people left standing at the gravesite.

"I can't believe he lied that much," Kristina said finally.

I raised my eyebrows in response. "What do you mean? He was lying?" Had I guessed right about his true feelings?

Kristina laughed and turned to us. "Yes. You mean you couldn't tell? He and Elijah hated each other. Well, honestly, I think he hated Elijah much more. Elijah barely paid him any attention, but he found him to be a weasel half the time. I figured Quincy would show up here to express his condolences, but I didn't think he'd lie so blatantly in front of you. Who was he trying to convince?"

That was a good question. Was he putting on a show for everyone, pretending to be heartbroken about Elijah's death, while secretly trying to cozy up to his ex-wife? Was this all a scheme to convince Kristina that she should take him up on his offer to help? Or was he hiding a guilty conscience by putting on this caring mask?

"Why would he say all those things in front of you?" Chrissy asked. "Wouldn't he know that you would know he's lying?"

"Not necessarily. I don't think he realizes how much I know about his relationship with Elijah. Elijah always talked about how much he could tell Quincy hated him, but I didn't necessarily see Quincy treat him that way. Quincy might think that Elijah only said good things about him, even if he was lying. Or he might think that we all believe the charade because that's easier. It's hard to say, but I'm surprised he laid it on so thick."

"It is strange," I noted. "Why would he lie unless he wants people to think they were closer than they actually were?"

Kristina's eyes widened and she leaned towards me. "This must mean he's the killer, right? Why lie, except to hide the truth about what he did? He and Elijah must've gotten into some kind of argument, and now Quincy is hiding the truth from everyone. Should we tell the police about this?"

Kristina had made some leaps, but I wasn't so sure if she was on the right track. Yes, it was strange that Quincy had lied about his feelings about Elijah, but many people lie. It didn't make them killers. He might have felt bad about how he treated Elijah in the past and wanted to pretend that they were actually much closer than they were. It was impossible to say why he did what he did, but it did raise some questions.

"I'm not so sure," I said finally. "It's something to keep in mind, though. If he reaches out to you again, will you let us know?" I wasn't convinced either way about Quincy's innocence, but I'd keep an eye on him just in case.

"Well, I'm glad you're looking into all of this." Kristina took my hands. "I know you didn't know Elijah, but I think you would've liked him, and I know he'd appreciate what you're doing for him now." She turned to Chrissy. "I'm sorry this is how we have to see each other again after so long, but I'm glad you were able to come. I have to stay down here for a little while, but let's not be strangers, okay?"

"Of course," Chrissy said. "Let me know if there's anything you need from me. I'm not exactly sure when I'm going back to California, but I'll be around if I can help in any way."

"Thank you. Please keep me updated on everything. If there's anything I can do to help, let me know."

She gave the three of us hugs, and we followed after the mourners who were heading back to the church. Kristina stayed behind to talk to the pastor.

We trudged up the path to the church and parking lot, my mind running over everything I'd learned so far. Why was Quincy lying? Was he the killer? Had Kristina lied to us today? I couldn't take her off my list of suspects simply because she'd been kind. Were her claims about reconciliation between her and Elijah true? If they were, then she had no reason to want him dead. But if she wasn't the killer, then who?

The three of us headed to my car in the parking lot. "Estelle, do you need a ride?" I asked her.

"Yes, please," she said, hopping into the backseat. "Now I don't have to pay for a taxi back home."

Chrissy and I climbed in front, and I began the drive back to Pine Brook and the inn.

"What did you think of her?" Chrissy asked as we drove.

"Well, Kristina's the second person to confirm that there was someone out there that Elijah feared. There's a good chance that this stalker is his killer." I paused, chewing on the inside of my cheek. "Do you think Quincy would know if a student was stalking Elijah? Would he even tell me if I asked?"

"If you tell him your name is Samantha again, maybe he'll listen," Chrissy said, her tone joking. Estelle chuckled from the backseat.

I huffed and gripped the steering wheel tighter. She was right. I wasn't likely to get more information out of Quincy, not after lying to him so blatantly. I didn't want to give him the opportunity to confront me about why I'd lied to him. Better to keep my distance and leave the sleuthing to the police.

14

"I hope Kristina's going to be okay tonight," Chrissy said as we filed into the warm inn together. "I can't imagine losing your husband like this, even if they were divorced. I always liked Kristina."

"She did seem nice," I agreed. "She's got a pretty solid alibi, too—she was driving across a bridge when Elijah was killed. I might still keep her on my list of suspects, though. I wonder if there's a way to fake something like that."

"Thanks for coming to this with me," Chrissy said, pulling Estelle and me into hugs. "This would've been much harder to do without you there. I think I'm going to go upstairs and call Mark. It'd be nice to have a quiet night in."

Thank goodness she was finally agreeing to speak with her husband. As far as I knew, they'd only talked once since their big fight. She must've regretted coming down here in the first place, given everything that ended up happening. Maybe he could give her some legal advice, too.

"Let me know if I can bring you anything."

We said our goodbyes, and she left the lobby, leaving Estelle and me to watch after her.

"So, what do you think?" Estelle asked.

"About what?" I hadn't realized she'd said anything.

"Please pay attention when I'm hunting criminals! We can't have any slip-ups if we're going to save your sister. I said I thought Kristina told us more than I expected, and without much prompting from you. It seems a little fishy to me."

"Well, she wasn't telling strangers—she knows Chrissy, and I told her I wanted to find out what happened to Elijah." Estelle tended to think everyone was a little fishy.

"What do you think about the stalker she mentioned?" I asked. "It lines up with what that realtor told me. Any idea who it might be?"

Estelle shrugged. "No clue. You might need to go back to the college and dig around a bit. See who seems more interested in Elijah's death than they should be."

I kept my mouth shut about the fact that one could argue that *we* were more interested in Elijah's death than we should be. She'd simply say that we were sleuthing, and therefore it was different.

"What about you? Did you find anything else out about the case?" I knew Estelle had done some of her own digging.

"I convinced Miriam to talk to me again, though she made me swear not to repeat this to anyone else. The police think Elijah was meeting someone behind Cheesy Does It, and they must've gotten into some kind of argument. She said they've consulted with a tread mark specialist to look at the scene, so Miriam thinks he might have been run over by a car, and they want to compare the tire marks found on the ground and his body."

If the killer had used their car to murder Elijah, that meant they didn't have to be strong; they used the strength of their car to kill him. Kristina was staying on my suspects list until further notice.

Estelle noticed the time on the grandfather clock in the lobby. "Oh, I am starving. I didn't eat before the funeral. I'm going to see if Hank has anything left from the lunch rush. Care to join me?"

Images of Elijah's dead body were floating through my brain, and I wasn't in the mood for food right now. I waved her off, promising to check in later.

A few minutes passed as I stood at the front desk, shuffling through the mail and staring around the lobby. I didn't know where Tracy was. Probably digging through a box of old junk, searching for something that would put the inn on the antique collectors' map. She was very determined to find us something to bring to the antiques fair. Had she found any other apartments for me to look at? I wasn't in a rush to leave the inn.

The lobby was quiet. Normally, I appreciated the silence, as it gave me some time to decompress from the stress of customer service, but now, all I could think about was Elijah's violent death.

Who hated someone enough to run them over with a car? Or had it been a convenient choice rather than a passion-filled choice? If the killer was smaller than Elijah, using their car may have been their only option.

The inn's doors opened as a *whoosh* of air entered the lobby, followed by a woman. She was short and Chinese, with straight dark hair hanging down her back, heavily made-up eyes, and a gold hoop sticking out of her nose. She kept glancing around the lobby as she approached the front desk. Her dark hair had purple streaks throughout.

"Are you Simone?" she asked.

Strange for her to know my name. Guests didn't usually,

and I didn't recognize her from around town. She looked young, though, no older than twenty.

"Yes, that's me," I said, straightening up to attention. "Are you checking in?"

She shook her head. "No, I'm here to get some details about something that happened earlier this week. Do you mind if I ask you some questions?"

She plopped her bright orange backpack on the desk in front of us and unzipped it, pulling things out of it. She removed a laptop, an iPad, hair scrunchies, a water bottle, a stack of tarot cards, two notebooks, a half-eaten apple, a doll with its head removed, and a damp rag. The woman piled all of this on the front desk between us, before finding a small notebook with glitter all over it. She shoved everything else back into her bag and pulled a pen out of her pocket, flipping open the notebook and looking up at me expectantly.

"Um," I said, clearing my throat and straightening up again. I'd been so focused on all the things she was carrying around in her backpack, I'd forgotten her question. Who walks around with a doll without a head?

"Sure," I said finally. "What's this about?"

"I'm investigating the murder of Elijah Norris," she said, scribbling a note in her notebook and standing up straighter, though I still towered over her. "I understand you were the one to find his body?"

I nodded, narrowing my eyes. Who exactly was this? "Yes, that's right," I said. "Sorry, are you with the police?"

I figured the answer was no, unless the police had started hiring teenagers with facial jewelry, but I had to ask.

She glanced at me over her notebook, then quickly back down again when I made eye contact. "Not quite. My name is Wanda Chen. I was...a friend of Elijah's, and I'm looking into his murder."

Well, now I felt like a jerk, acting suspicious of the friend of a dead man.

"I'm so sorry for your loss. I'm happy to help, but I really think you should leave this to the police." I ignored the nagging voice in my head that reminded me that I didn't leave these kinds of things to the police. This woman was a child, practically, so it was different.

"The police are incompetent and barking up all kinds of wrong trees," she spat out.

Patel deserved more credit than that, but I kept quiet as I had thought those same things about Tate myself.

"I'm here to make sure they find the right killer," Wanda went on. "I understand your sister was with you when you found the body. Is she here? Can I talk to her?"

"No, I'm sorry, she's not available. Any questions you have, I can answer." I wasn't interested in subjecting Chrissy to this pseudo-detective.

Wanda went through some crazy spiel, not really making sense but trying to seem professional and serious. As her questions progressed, my suspicions started rising and rising.

"Wait, how exactly did you know Elijah? You said you were a friend? Where did you two meet?"

"At...at the college," she said, keeping her gaze down. "It doesn't matter where we met. Where were you two nights ago? I have reason to believe someone broke into his office and stole something. Can anyone vouch for your whereabouts?"

They met at the college? The truth dawned on me like a beacon of light. Was this Elijah's stalker I'd been hearing all about? Would she tell me the truth if I came out and asked it?

"Were you at his funeral today? I didn't see you there."

"No, it was a private event. I wasn't invited," Wanda said before she could stop herself. She smacked her hand across her mouth as if to grab the words out of the air and shove them back inside and looked up at me with wide eyes.

"Did Elijah consider you a friend?" I put my hands on my hips, leaning across the desk. "I've heard all about you, Wanda. He was afraid of you. He was going to leave town because he didn't like that you were around."

"That's not true!" she said, balling her hands into fists and smacking the front desk. "He loved me! He just didn't know it yet!"

"It's all right." I held up my hands in what I hoped was a placating gesture. "I didn't mean to upset you. Why don't you tell me about him?"

Wanda sighed, her voice softening and her shoulders curving inwards as if to protect herself. "I took a class with him my freshman year." Her voice was soft, her energy down as she remembered that time. "That's when we first met. He was so smart and passionate and kind. I took other classes with him after that year, including an independent study. I wanted to spend all my time with him."

"I heard he was an excellent teacher. It sounds like he went above and beyond to help his students."

"He did! He was so much better than all the boys in my classes. He could talk about real things. And I could tell he wanted to spend time with me, too. He brought me books to read and told me about articles he thought I'd like."

This was starting to sound like a teacher who was maybe a little too interested in his students.

"And then, one day, it all changed," Wanda went on. "He wouldn't answer my calls and stopped talking to me in the hallway. I...I found out where he lived, and I went by one day to see if he was okay. But he wouldn't talk to me." She hung her head as if ashamed by his actions or by hers, I couldn't quite tell.

"Then, all the students got an email from the department that he's dead," she continued. "An email! We didn't even have a chance to make up. I thought he really cared about me."

She was crying now, and I passed her a tissue from behind the desk.

My heart broke for her. Clearly she'd developed a crush on the man, and maybe Elijah had even encouraged it, bringing her books and articles, but he must've realized that it was getting inappropriate and tried to put a stop to it. Why did he tell people he had a stalker, though? Yes, showing up at his house was out of line, but the sense I'd gotten from others was that Wanda was obsessed with him. Had Elijah played up the story to protect himself in case Wanda ever went to the college about what happened? Or was she lying to me, too?

"I'm so sorry about this," I said, desperate to get at the truth. "I'm trying to find his killer, too. Maybe we can help each other?"

"I just want you to answer my questions, not get in my way," Wanda said, her voice now harsh. "You better stay out of this. First his ex-wife, now you. And that gross professor from the department. All of you need to leave me alone. I will find his killer, all on my own." Wanda stormed out of the inn without a backward glance.

Gross professor? Was she talking about Quincy? And when had she interacted with Kristina?

I ran to the door after Wanda, wanting to see what kind

of car she drove. Maybe the police could match the tire treads on her car with what they found at the crime scene.

Instead, Wanda climbed into the backseat of a cab. Drat. Well, there went that theory. Maybe she wasn't driving her car because she'd just used it to kill a man. I'd make sure to ask Patel about any cars registered in Wanda's name.

Was Wanda Elijah's stalker? Did she kill him? After talking to Estelle, it was clear the killer didn't need to be a big, strong person. Could Wanda have hit him with her car? Or would Wanda be the one to find Elijah's killer?

15

"You're a lifesaver, Eddy." Chrissy smiled up at the server gratefully.

"Not a problem, doll." He winked at us.

The next morning, a Monday, Chrissy and I had met for breakfast in the bistro. She'd spent the night up in her room, not interested in being asked about Elijah's death or getting taken into the police station for questioning. As much as she loved crime shows, she was quickly learning how much worse it was to live through one of those shows.

She sipped the coffee, content, already beginning to wake up. Hank's coffee was known to have healing powers; it had gotten me through many boring meetings with vendors at the inn.

I reached across the table and squeezed her hand. "I'm glad you made it down for breakfast."

Elijah's funeral had been tough for her to see yesterday. The bags under her eyes had deepened. How much sleep had she gotten last night?

"I'm just grateful for this." She held up the mug, chugging down the coffee.

"Slow down there. The caffeine in that will hit you like a freight train."

"Sorry." She set the mug down. "I'm feeling a little frazzled, and this is helping me to feel normal. I was up kind of late last night. I talked to Mark and Hannah. She's back from staying with Mark's parents, and she said her class is doing a performance of *Five Little Turkeys* next month. She's got a small part, but she wanted to know when I'd be back to see it." She looked down into her mug, as if her departing flight would show up in her coffee dregs.

"How did it go with Mark?" I asked slowly. "Do you think you might be ready to go back soon?"

While it had been nice to have Chrissy around for a few days, her family clearly needed her at home. The police might not appreciate her leaving, but she did have a family to take care of.

"I know I haven't talked to Elijah in years," she said, "but he was an important part of my life at one time. It hurts my heart to know his life has come to an end this way because of someone else. It doesn't feel right to leave until this case is solved." Emotion choked her words. "Lord knows I've watched enough *Forensic Files* and *Datelines* in my life; maybe it's time I put all that knowledge to use and help you and the police figure out who did this to Elijah."

I shouldn't have been surprised; she'd had a million questions for me when I'd found my first body last month, and she'd always been obsessed with true crime stories. Still, was this urge to stay solely because she was fascinated by the crime, or was she hiding something else from me about her feelings?

"You can stay around as long as you'd like. Someone here is clearly happy about it." I motioned to the side of the table, where Lola was sitting on the ground. She was staring up adoringly at Chrissy, who laughed and reached down to ruffle the beagle's ears.

I could handle Chrissy's visit for a few more days. The anxiety I'd felt when she'd first arrived—rooted in my insecurities about my inability to run the inn—had dissipated over the course of her visit. Of course, now it was replaced by anxiety related to the fact that there was a murderer running around town. Chrissy had always supported me over the years, even letting me crash on her couch for a few months when I was eighteen and still trying to figure out what I wanted out of life. I could handle her hanging around the inn for a few days.

"How was your talk with Mark? Did he have any legal advice for you?"

"Mostly the same as what Ron already told us," Chrissy said, sipping her coffee. "He said to keep quiet here with you. I didn't mention you've been sleuthing. Not sure if he'd approve."

She was probably right about that. Hopefully, this all wouldn't be a waste of time, and we'd be able to help the police find Elijah's killer.

We put in our breakfast order with Eddy and happily accepted a refill of coffee. The other tables were filling up, and the chattering of guests gave me a chance to clear my mind and think about the last few days.

"What do you think about Quincy?" Chrissy asked. "He acted strangely at the funeral, didn't he?"

"Yes, but the more I think about it, the less likely it seems that he killed Elijah. For one thing, he was teaching in front of a bunch of students."

"True." Chrissy's voice was thoughtful. "Do you think the police have confirmed that?"

"Maybe. I'd guess they would've arrested him already if

they discovered he was lying. Probably, Quincy was simply jealous of Elijah and is now grateful he's gone. I don't think he's a cold-blooded murderer."

"Kristina seemed pretty upset at the funeral. I haven't seen her in years, so it's hard to know if she was hiding something. Do you think she's covering up her real feelings?"

I shrugged. "I don't know. She shared a lot of information with us—was that solely because she hopes we'll find Elijah's killer, or was she trying to lead us in a different direction away from her? Her alibi appears strong, though. It's hard to fake a trip over a toll bridge."

"Maybe she knows someone who works for the bridge who could fudge the records for her?"

"The police would probably discover that sort of fraud. Seems like a hard thing to cover up. But maybe you're right —I'm keeping her on my list."

Eddy dropped off our breakfast orders and we quickly dug in. I'd gone with an omelet this morning, while Chrissy had chosen pancakes and fresh fruit. Hank was a master in the kitchen, even with something as simple as breakfast food.

"Oh, I forgot to tell you," I said around mouthfuls of egg. "Elijah's stalker visited the inn yesterday."

Chrissy let out a gasp so loud, several patrons at other tables looked our way. I quickly shushed her.

"Will you calm down?"

"Why wouldn't you tell me about this immediately?" she hissed, keeping her voice down. "I thought we were investigating this together. And now you wait twelve hours to give me this big clue?"

"Sorry. It's not that big of a deal. She was weird, but I don't know if she's the killer."

"Why do you say that?"

I quickly explained about Wanda's visit, making note of the strange things she'd pulled out of her bag, but also emphasizing the fact that it seemed like Elijah had led her on.

"It sounds like Wanda was young and fell in love with a nice, older man, who realized that they were closer than they should've been, so he started pulling away. But I'm not sure if that means she's a killer."

I'd sent all of this in a text message to Patel that morning. I didn't want to bias her against Wanda before she'd had a chance to talk to her, so I kept things vague. Patel could follow up with Wanda on her own and make her own assessment.

"She said he brought her books and things?" Chrissy asked, her voice soft.

I nodded. "It honestly sounded pretty inappropriate for a professor to be doing. It makes me question Elijah a bit, too, you know?"

"Listen, Simone, there's something I should tell you—" Chrissy started, but we were interrupted by Tracy.

"Guess what I found," she said, smirking wide, her hands on her hips as she looked down at the two of us.

"Another vase?" I asked halfheartedly. I wasn't in the mood to *ooh* and *aah* over another piece of ceramic from T.J. Maxx.

"Another apartment! This one's perfect." Her grin was at full-wattage now, her eyes bright with glee.

I groaned. "Come on, we just got done seeing those atrocious apartments. You really want to make me go through that again?"

"This place is so much better! Two bedrooms, a beautiful kitchen, and the bathrooms are totally in their own rooms."

I rolled my eyes. "That's not really a selling point; that should happen by default."

"Look, I promise this place is amazing. You have to trust me!"

"Let's go look at this place," Chrissy said. "You said you need to get out of that suite, right? So you can open it up to guests? You should look at anything that seems like a good fit. Plus, bathrooms in their own rooms? How can you turn that down?" She smiled to let me know she was joking, and I returned the grin.

"What the hell?" I said finally. "Let's go see it."

The rain had cleared up the night before and the day was sunny, though cold. We bundled up in jackets and climbed into Tracy's car.

Tracy explained that the apartment was located in a building just about a ten-minute drive from the inn. So, while my commute would be longer, it wouldn't be awful.

We pulled up in front of a plain, four-story building, with tall trees lining every available space. The lobby was drab, with dim lighting and a sad-looking fern in the corner. Was this already a mistake?

We climbed up two flights of stairs, as the elevator was out of commission. Tracy promised me that it worked the majority of the time, and I pondered whether I could ever have an apartment where the elevator worked all of the time.

She knocked on the door to 2B and we were welcomed in by a man wearing ironed jeans and a tucked in, button-down shirt. I held in my irritation as I realized how much of a waste this trip was turning out to be. No way could someone in ironed jeans show me anything good.

All that was wiped from my brain as we shuffled into the apartment and stood in the living room.

The place had floor-to-ceiling windows against the far wall, which let in the dazzling morning light. Hardwood floors throughout, and the furniture was staged in a beautifully minimalist touch. Tall bookshelves were built into the side walls. Images of all the books I could buy flashed across my eyes.

We followed ironed jeans into the kitchen, which was larger than my bedroom in L.A., with gleaming appliances, a huge fridge, and a small dining nook in the corner, with a tall window looking out onto a backyard on the lower level.

The two bedrooms were spacious; the first was designed to look like an office, and I pictured all the inn business I could get done here. The second room was large enough to fit a king-size bed. I didn't have the money for a king-size bed right now, but as I dreamt of all that space, I figured I could make it work. The two bathrooms were sleek, with gorgeous sinks and tubs. And the rent was perfect for what I could afford.

Back in the living room, Tracy looked up at me expectantly and I turned to the landlord.

"Where should I apply?" I asked him, and Chrissy squealed.

"I'm so happy you loved it!" Chrissy said as we shuffled down the stairs back to the lobby.

"I told you we'd find something great," Tracy added.

"You're right, you're right, it's perfect," I told her. "I just hope I get it." I'd filled out an application before we left, and the landlord promised he'd get back to me soon.

"Is there some party in my building, and no one invited me?" Nick stood at the mailboxes in the lobby, smiling.

"Simone is thinking about renting 2B," Tracy told him.

Nick's face lit up at those words. "Is that right?" he asked me. "I'm in 3B. I guess we'll be neighbors."

"Well, I still need to get the apartment," I said slowly. "I'm sure there's a lot of competition for these units."

"Did Miguel show you the place?" he asked, naming the landlord. "He's a softie. I'll go put in a good word for you." He waved goodbye and loped up the stairs, presumably going to talk me up to Miguel, my new landlord.

"I don't know about this," I said as we walked out of the building. Tracy and Chrissy looked at me in surprise.

"What are you talking about?" Chrissy asked.

"You just said this place was great," Tracy said.

"I know, I know, but can I really live in the same building as one of my vendors? He's practically an employee!"

Plus, he made my stomach tingle every time he came near, but I kept that to myself.

"Besides, what if we get into a fight and he stops supplying produce to the inn, and then I have to see him every day?" I went on. "This could be bad for the inn's business."

Tracy rolled her eyes. "You're being ridiculous. You're going to move into this apartment and be so happy that I found this place for you, and that's final."

She stomped back to her car and climbed in, done with the conversation.

Chrissy smiled. "Those bathrooms were pretty amazing. Did you check out the tubs?"

They were right. I was being silly to pass up on this apartment. I linked arms with Chrissy and led us back to

Tracy's car, ignoring the butterflies in my stomach that still hadn't let up since seeing Nick. This was all fine.

BACK AT THE INN, a couple of guests were standing at the front desk. Nadia was nowhere in sight, so I hurried over to deal with the guests while Tracy went to take Lola for a walk.

"Checking out?" I asked, sliding behind the front desk.

"Yes," the man said, passing along the key to their room. Room II—the Montgomerys. They'd checked in with their eight-year-old son—who was currently playing with a choo choo train on the ground—at the beginning of the weekend.

"We had a lovely stay," the wife said, leaning across the counter. "It's not often we can take a weekend away anywhere, but this has been wonderful."

I smiled as I tallied up their receipts, noting the late-night orders of chicken wings from the bistro, and passed them the bill to sign.

"Well, we'd love to have you back whenever you can make it," I said. "And tell your friends, too!"

"We heard all about the dreadful murder," the husband said, leaning in close and lowering his voice. "At that cheesy restaurant?"

I nodded, but didn't say anything. I wasn't interested in gossiping with two Nosey Nellies from out of town.

"Who do you think did it?" the woman asked, signing the bill and passing along her credit card.

"No clue," I said with a smile, swiping her card and passing it back. "You all have a great drive home."

They paused for a moment, as if waiting for me to say something more about the murder, then called for their son and picked up their bags. I waited until their backs were turned to the desk before rolling my eyes. People couldn't help but be interested in murder, could they?

"Simone? Could we talk for a moment?" Chrissy approached the front desk, fiddling with the hem of her shirt.

"Sure. What's up?" I'd thought she'd gone upstairs to her room after coming back from the apartment, but it looked like she'd been down in the lobby the whole time.

"There's something I need to tell you." She took a deep breath, keeping her gaze down low. "I lied to you, before. I...I went to see Elijah, the day before he died."

16

My brain felt like it was moving through sludge as I tried to process Chrissy's words. She'd gone to see Elijah? When? How?

Chrissy hurried on, before I could ask any questions. "We'd been talking before I came down here. I found him on Facebook and messaged him about meeting up once I realized he lived so close to you. Mark and I have been fighting, and we got into a huge fight right before I left. I...I was thinking about leaving him. That's why I came up here so suddenly. I wanted to get away from Mark, and I wanted to talk to Elijah. I went to his apartment the night after we saw him in the bistro. That's why I wasn't here at the inn."

My responsible, overachiever sister was planning to leave her husband and had run away to an ex-boyfriend's house, and now that ex-boyfriend was dead and the police suspected her of murder. Saying it to myself, it sounded like a TV show. But it was all real, and it was happening right now.

"But then you told me all that stuff about Wanda, about Elijah giving her books and treating her special," Chrissy went on hurriedly. "And I realized he was playing me, too. I don't want to keep lying."

Elijah's neighbors had probably seen Chrissy at his house, and maybe the police had found her fingerprints. That must've been why Patel had questioned her so intensely. I couldn't believe Chrissy had been keeping this from me. What else was she lying about?

"I know you're upset with me, and I'm sorry for lying," Chrissy said. "I'm just really scared. I don't want to go to jail."

She broke down then, tears streaming down her face. I pulled her close, making shushing sounds to comfort her. How could I believe that she was still lying to me? Yes, she'd kept some things from me, but she was also faced with a challenging situation. The only way we were going to get out of this is if I believed her.

"All right, you need to stay here," I said finally, pulling away from the hug. "No more talking about sleuthing, or even thinking about sleuthing. We can't give the police any more ammo against you. I think it's probably best if you go upstairs now."

She nodded, her cheeks wet. "I'm so sorry." She wiped at her face and hurried up the stairs.

What was I supposed to do now? Should I tell Patel what Chrissy had told me?

No, that seemed like a bad idea. I didn't want to bring evidence against my sister straight to the police. Patel would be upset if she knew I was keeping this from her, but I couldn't betray Chrissy like that. The best thing I could do right now would be to find Elijah's killer before the police arrested my sister. But what should I do next?

According to Vivian, Elijah had also been looking for a new apartment before he died, but it didn't seem like he'd moved recently, which meant he was still at the house that Wanda had gone to visit. The police had probably already searched his home, but maybe there was something they'd missed. I'd told Patel I was going to stay out of her investigation, but knowing what I now knew about Chrissy, I had to get involved.

Once there was a lull in the guests, I called up Kristina before I could talk myself out of it.

"Elijah's house? Sure, I'll text you the address." Her tone on the line turned suspicious. "Why do you ask?"

The lie fell from my tongue easily. "I'm trying to figure out why he would've come to Pine Brook to look for a new place. It'll help to put his apartment on the map and see how far away it is."

It was a lame excuse, but she seemed to believe me as my phone buzzed with a new text.

Address in hand, I planned my next move. Nadia had come back to the front desk, having just finished folding laundry in the laundry room.

"Did I miss a rush of guests?" she asked me. "Oops."

I scoffed. "Yeah, like you didn't bolt to the laundry room as soon as they showed up. It's fine, but I need you to stay here for a little while, okay?"

She nodded, slouching against the countertop and pulling out her phone to text her boyfriend. I rolled my eyes but held my tongue. I couldn't begrudge someone in love, could I?

I didn't want to go snooping alone, but I definitely couldn't bring Chrissy along with me. If the police found us hanging around Elijah's house, who knew what they would think? Fortunately, I had someone else I could call.

Turning away from the front desk, I whipped out my phone and sent a text to Estelle. She was back within seconds, her emoji-filled response reflecting her enthusiasm. Looks like we were on for some snooping tonight.

"Are you ready?" Estelle asked, eager to leap out of the car.

She'd pulled on a black beanie to cover her white hair and was wearing black jeans and a black hoodie. I hadn't had time to change, but fortunately my raincoat was black, and I zipped it up to cover the blue shirt I was wearing.

We were parked across the street from Elijah's house, staring out the car window. The rain had picked up on our drive over, and the sun had fully set. As I drove, the seriousness of what we were doing had come over me, and I'd begun to question this illegal activity.

"All right, no breaking in," I said, turning to Estelle. "We're just here to look. We can peek through the windows, but we can't commit a crime. Agreed?"

"Agreed," Estelle huffed out, clearly upset about her lost opportunity to smash a window.

We climbed out of my car, glancing up and down the street. The rain at least covered most of the sound of our footsteps, and we figured most people would stay inside their houses on a night like this, not likely to go investigate if they saw anyone snooping around their dead neighbor's house. Of course, they might've been likely to just call the police if they saw something suspicious, so I sent up a tiny prayer that no one would look out their window.

This area of Holliston seemed nice enough, with single-family homes up and down the street. Oak trees lined the sidewalk, giving the impression that this neighborhood had been around for generations.

Elijah's house was set back from the curb, with a small

yard in front. It looked like he planted vegetables up here, though many were getting soaked through from the rain. The house was dark, but a small path led around the side of the house, so I motioned to Estelle and we headed back that way. It seemed better to get out from in front of the house, than continue standing in the street.

There wasn't much more back here. He had another small yard, this time with flowers blooming all throughout. I hadn't pictured him as someone with a green thumb. What did I really know about him, though, besides what others had told me? Everyone had hidden sides.

"I don't know what to look for," I said to Estelle, staring around and trying to get some inspiration.

"Me either," she said, seeming resigned to that fact. "It doesn't seem right to try to break into his house like this. It feels like we're disturbing something sacred by coming to a dead man's home."

"Maybe we should just leave," I said, turning to face her and jumping at the sight of a man entering the yard.

"Sorry to scare you," he called out, waving his hands and smiling. "I saw you coming back and wanted to make sure everything was okay."

I nudged Estelle to keep her quiet and waved back at the man. "You didn't scare us. Just surprised to see someone here," I called out. "We're friends of Kristina, and she asked us to stop by and make sure everything was okay back here with the garden." The lie fell out of my mouth, and I didn't hesitate with it.

The man looked to be about Elijah's age, maybe a little older. He was short, with acne-scarred skin, a bulbous nose, and sandy blonde hair that was beginning to thin. He was wearing a long trench coat, and his nice shoes squished in the grass as he approached.

"Oh yes, I've been meaning to pop over to Kristina's and see how she's doing. I wasn't able to make it to the funeral, so I wanted to pay my condolences. My name is Marcus." He smiled, his features softening as he did, and held out his hand for us to shake.

We introduced ourselves and shook his hand, and I wondered what he was really doing here. We definitely weren't here for respectable reasons, so how could he be?

"How did you know Elijah?" Estelle asked, jumping in when I didn't say anything.

"We're old friends," Marcus said. "We go way back. I was out of town in Vegas when I heard about the news, so I rushed right back as soon as I could."

"At a bachelor party?" I asked. Why else would a grown man be in Las Vegas in the winter?

Marcus turned his gaze on me, a chill going through me at the sight of his eyes. They were dark and dead-looking.

"I'm a bookie. I've got some business in Vegas these days."

Estelle frowned, like she didn't buy his story or his reason for being here, either. We didn't say anything.

"Well," Marcus said to break the silence. "It's getting pretty dark out here, and it looks like all these vegetables are taken care of." He gestured around to the yard. "Why don't we head out, and you can tell me more about how you know Elijah and Kristina. Maybe we can stop by her place together?"

I grabbed Estelle's arm and started shuffling down the path. "Actually, we have dinner plans we need to make. But it was lovely meeting you. I'll be sure to tell Kristina we ran into you the next time we see her." I waved at Marcus and hustled Estelle out of the yard.

We climbed into my car and I waved at Marcus again as he eventually got into his own car and drove away.

"What was that all about?" Estelle asked. "Who was that man?"

"I don't know, but I'm going to find out."

I turned on the car's engine and peeled away from the curb, following after Marcus.

17

M y hands thrummed against the steering wheel as we drove, street lights blinking on as we passed them. Marcus pulled off Elijah's residential street quickly and moved into the flow of traffic on the main part of Holliston. I let out the breath I hadn't realized I'd been holding. I'd been worried about him spotting us, which would've been easy to do while on the residential streets. Not many people were out right now, given the weather and the darkening sky.

On the main drag of Holliston, however, I could let one or two cars separate us and still keep him in view. I glanced out the window as the town went by, trying to see street signs to get a sense of where we were and where we were going.

"Who is this guy?" Estelle asked, peering through the windshield.

She was bouncing in her seat with energy. A high-speed chase was probably exactly what she thought was missing from her life these days.

"I don't know," I said, focusing back on the road in front of me.

Marcus took a turn and we followed after him after a beat, then crept behind him as he took the onramp to the freeway. The sign stated we were heading north, away from Pine Brook. How much longer would we have to follow him for?

"I don't buy what he said about how he knows Elijah," Estelle said. "You could tell he was lying. Do you think he killed Elijah?"

I paused for a moment, taking in her words. I stared at Marcus' bumper, looking for blood, but that was probably something you got cleaned up quickly so no one could verify it.

"I don't know," I said, shaking my head to clear my thoughts. "I wish we knew who he was. Where is he going now? When did he really get into town?"

Estelle gave a little squeal and pulled out her phone, tapping in a number. "I have an idea," she said, holding the phone up to her ear.

"What?" I asked, but she shushed me and focused on the phone.

"Meredith? It's Estelle. How are you, dear?"

The other person on the line, presumably this Meredith, said a few words, and Estelle laughed.

"That is too true. We'll have to get together soon. Listen, I was wondering if you could help me with something. I'm in Holliston, and I'm with a man who claims to be a bookie from Las Vegas." She paused as Meredith spoke. "Oh yes, dear, I know! What will these kids get up to next? But listen, I'm wondering if you can run a search on him. I've got his license plate right in front of me." She rattled off the numbers. "Thanks, Meredith, you're a doll. Call me as soon as you get a hit."

She murmured her goodbyes and hung up the phone, slipping it back into her purse and looking as pleased as the cat with a canary in its mouth.

"What was that all about?" I asked.

"A friend at the DMV. She just got the job. She can look up any license plate for me."

I narrowed my eyes at her. "Is that legal?"

Estelle shrugged, looking innocent. "Why, I don't know, dear. Meredith never said it was illegal."

Her eyes twinkled, and I groaned. Great. Now I could add getting someone fired to the list of things Estelle had talked me into. Not to mention the trouble we'd get into for using government computers to spy on a man who could be completely innocent. Was this a federal offense? Who'd take care of Lola if I ended up in federal prison with daredevil Estelle?

"Don't worry about it," Estelle said. "Just drive. Meredith has been there a week; I'm sure she's got a handle on things. Besides, I'll keep your name out of it."

I appreciated the thought and tried to ignore the pit in my stomach. Hopefully, Marcus would stop driving soon, and we could figure out who he was and where he was going, then get out of here before he spotted us. I'd never tailed someone like this, but I'd seen it on a lot of TV shows, so I tried to emulate those I'd seen on the screen. He'd have to stop eventually, right? He wasn't driving all the way back to Vegas, was he?

A buzzing in the console between us broke into my thoughts. Tracy was calling. I swore.

"Can you grab that?" I asked Estelle. "Put it on speaker

and be quiet." I didn't want to admit to Tracy what we were doing, given that it might be illegal.

"Hey, Tracy, what's up?" I asked once the phone was on, trying to keep my voice steady.

"Hey, I just saw your sister moping around, and I wanted to make sure everything was okay."

In the chaos of this high-speed chase, I'd managed to forget all about Chrissy's lies.

"Yeah, I think she's just tired, that's all," I said. "Will you keep an eye on her for me?"

"Sure. Where are you? You sound weird."

"You're on speaker. I'm in the car with Estelle," I said, glancing over at the older woman.

"Hi, Tracy," Estelle trilled into the phone, sounding normal and not at all panicked—unlike me. "I'm sorry for keeping Simone out so late. I needed to pick up a prescription, and I don't like driving at night. Simone graciously offered to give me a lift."

"Oh, well that was nice of her," Tracy said, and I sent a silent thanks to Estelle for being such a magnificent liar. "Let me know when you're back." She hung up the phone and I let out a rush of air.

"Nice one," I told Estelle as she put my phone back in the console.

She grinned, looking mighty pleased with herself, and I tried not to think about all the times she might've been lying to me in the past.

Marcus had gotten off the freeway, and we were now driving through Tacoma. At least he wasn't planning on going all the way to Vegas tonight. Tacoma was busier than Holliston, and I settled in to follow along behind him.

At that moment, my phone buzzed again. This time Detective Patel's name flashed across the screen. I swore again, louder. Why were all these people calling me now? I needed to focus on the road in front of me and the potential killer getting away.

"Answer it, please," I told Estelle, gritting myself for what was about to come.

"Simone, I tried to find you at the inn but Tracy said you were out." Patel's voice came through the phone. "I spoke with Wanda today."

"Really? What did she say?" I asked, keeping my voice steady.

"Not much—she's weird, like you said—but we learned something else interesting."

"Oh?"

"I'm only telling you this because I don't want you going around telling people that Wanda is a killer," she said. "We've confirmed that Elijah was hit by a car, and Wanda doesn't drive. She doesn't have a license. She's got some fear of driving after a car accident when she was a kid."

That shut me up pretty quickly. Estelle had also said that Elijah was killed by a car, and it would be pretty hard for Wanda to get ahold of a car if she didn't have a license. Plus, if she did have a fear of driving, she wasn't likely to get behind the wheel. That would also explain why I saw her getting into a cab after she left the inn—she didn't have a car of her own.

"I won't tell anyone else about Wanda. I guess this puts us back at square one, huh?"

"Since you are not a part of this investigation, no, it does not put you back anywhere," she said, her voice stern. "Where are you right now? It sounds echoey."

"Driving. With Estelle. She, uh, she needed help getting a prescription."

I clearly needed some lessons from Estelle on lying.

Patel paused for a beat and I worried she was about to call me out.

"Tell her I said hello. And you might want to get back to the inn soon. I saw your sister and she looked pretty rough." She said her goodbyes and hung up, and Estelle put the phone back in the console.

"Turn it on silent," I told her. "I'd rather not get interrupted again."

Particularly now because Marcus had pulled into the parking lot of a warehouse. I drove past the building and found a parking spot several yards away. Marcus got out of his car and looked around, and Estelle and I dove down into our seats. Fortunately, he didn't spot us. He tied his jacket tighter around himself and strode into the building.

Estelle and I settled into our seats to wait and see what would happen next. We were deep in Tacoma now, but I didn't recognize any of the streets. There were commercial buildings to our left, a few shops and stores, and a set of residential apartments on the next block. A homeless person walked down the street, a thick blanket wrapped around her shoulders. I hoped she was going someplace warm for the night.

"What do you think he's doing in there?" Estelle asked.

"I don't know," I said, staring out the window.

After Marcus had entered the warehouse and shut the door, the street was quiet. What was he up to?

An hour passed. Estelle and I initially had the radio on, but the songs kept repeating themselves, and we couldn't agree on a station, so we turned it off. Estelle tried to come up with a game for us to play, but she kept forgetting the rules. We were not prepared for a long stakeout, but I didn't want to leave in case Marcus came out and led us someplace that pointed to his guilt.

"Do you think he's going to leave anytime soon?" Estelle asked, but before I had a chance to answer, someone tapped against the driver's side window, and we both jumped.

Marcus was standing right outside my car!

18

Estelle and I took a couple of deep breaths. Marcus leaned down so he was looking right into the car and motioned for me to roll down the window. I hesitated, my instincts telling me to hit the gas and drive away, but maybe there was a way for this to look totally normal.

"Good evening." I started the car, rolled down the power window, just a smidge, and smiled up at him. I didn't want to give him an opportunity to reach his hand into the window and grab my throat.

"I thought I spotted someone following behind my car," Marcus said, leering into the window. "Just didn't realize it was two old biddies. Why the hell are you following me?"

"Following? We weren't following. We, uh, we're meeting someone at those apartments." I gestured to the building on the next block.

"Why are you sitting around in your car, then? Why don't you get outside and go see them? I'll walk you in. This neighborhood isn't very safe."

He stepped away from the door and held out his hands, a creepy smile on his face.

"Actually, we need to get going," I said, moving to roll up the window, but he was fast, and he slipped his elbow into the space between the window and the frame before I could roll it up.

"Now, you listen here," he said, glaring down into the car, any smile gone. "You stay away from me, and you stay away from my business, or else someone is about to get hurt. Now drive."

He stepped away from the car and I hit the gas, careening away from the curb.

We drove in silence, my hands shaking. At first, I'd been worried he'd call the police on me, and I'd have to explain to Patel what Estelle and I had been doing tonight. Now I was worried he was going to find me and run me over, just like he had with Elijah.

"He has to be the killer, right?" Estelle asked.

We'd been silent for the past few miles as I drove us back to Pine Brook. I'd been so focused on keeping my gaze on the road and trying to keep my mind empty that I'd almost forgotten Estelle was in the car with me. How dumb was it to bring her on this mission? We both could have been killed!

"What do you mean?" I asked, glancing over at her, her words slowly permeating my sluggish brain. I couldn't get the image of Marcus' looming, threatening form out of my head.

"Marcus!" she said, sounding exasperated. "He must be the killer, right? You don't just show up at a victim's home, drive to an abandoned warehouse, and then threaten the people following you, do you?"

If two people were following you, it seemed you might be likely to threaten them to get them to go away. But I didn't think Estelle would want to hear that take on it.

Just then, her phone chirped in her purse. She reached in and pulled it out, her eyes widening as she read the screen.

"Yes, Meredith, what is it?" she asked, hurriedly putting it on speakerphone.

"I looked up that license plate you sent me." Meredith's voice came through the phone, sounding far away. I glanced down at the phone Estelle was holding out; how old was this thing? Was it not used to sending calls from two towns over?

"What did you find out?" Estelle asked, not seeming to mind the quality of the call, so I focused back on Meredith's voice, too.

"Well, I had to expand my search, since the license plate you sent isn't registered in Washington state. I'm not really supposed to do this, but I was able to do another search in the Nevada DMV records. Marcus Hendricks owns the car you're following right now. I can't see much more besides his home address in Nevada and the fact that he has a bunch of unpaid parking tickets. It looks like his license plate was tagged speeding through a light on the route between Las Vegas and Pine Brook this week. I bet he's up here looking for someone who owes him money. That's what bookies do, right?" Meredith was talking fast, the words falling out of her mouth in a rush, like she wanted to quickly move past this potentially illegal thing she had done.

Why would a bookie from Las Vegas drive all the way to Pine Brook? It was a long drive; why hadn't he flown? He couldn't bring a gun on a plane unless it was licensed, but no one would check his car for a gun on that drive. Did he have a gun on him now?

"If you're looking for more information on him," Meredith went on, "you could do an online search with his name and see what comes up. I saw that on TV once."

"Thanks, Meredith, you're a doll," Estelle said. "Good tip about looking him up online. We'll go do that right now." She hung up and dropped her phone back into her bag. "Do you know what this means?"

"What?"

"We get to do an online search for a possible killer! How exciting is this?"

An online search didn't sound all that exciting to me, but Estelle's enthusiasm was infectious, and I cracked a smile.

"All right, let's go back to your place and see what we can find."

We pulled to a stop in front of Estelle's home and she dashed out of the car before the engine was even off, tapping away on her cell phone. I switched off the engine and unbuckled my seatbelt, but paused before climbing out after her.

Marcus' outburst was still drilled into my brain. Was he our killer? Or was he simply a creepy guy hanging around? The only way to find out was to follow after Estelle.

Miles was sitting in their front foyer when I entered, appearing to play a game of chess against himself.

"Who's winning?" I asked as I passed him.

"Who's winning?" He looked up, his eyes as wide as dollar coins, and gave a laugh after a moment. "Ah. I see. Yes, I'm recreating a game from earlier today. Someone at the park beat me, and I'm trying to figure out how they did it."

"Good luck. Don't mind us; we're just hunting for a killer."

Miles chuckled. "Good luck to you, as well. Don't let her go too crazy, will you? I'd still like to have a wife at the end of all this."

"No promises, but I'll try my best." I made my way into their living room while Miles returned to his game of chess against himself. Who would win in this head to head match?

"I found him!" Estelle was sitting on the couch, her phone gripped in her hand, and looked up at me with glee.

"How did you do that so fast?" I took a seat next to her and tried to catch a glimpse of her phone.

"Like Meredith said, I saw this on TV, too. You can do a public records search in different states. There's way too much stuff on the internet these days!"

"That's amazing." Since when was my friend so tech savvy? Maybe I should start watching these TV shows with her. "What did you find out?"

"He's got a rap sheet from New York that's as long as my arm, including assault, but he hasn't gotten into any trouble in Las Vegas. Meredith was right about that traffic ticket on the way up here; I can already see it on his record."

Estelle was right; there was way too much information available online. I hoped no one ever investigated me and tried to find all my dirty secrets from the past.

"Marcus has to be our killer!" Estelle was buzzing with excitement at what she had learned.

"I don't know," I said slowly. "Assault isn't murder, right?"

"It makes sense, though, doesn't it? Elijah owes Marcus money, and, rather than wait around for it, he drives all the way up here in one go to get it. But Elijah won't budge. He's a respected professor now; he can't have someone from his past showing up like this. He tells Marcus he won't pay, or maybe he asks to speak in the alley behind Cheesy Does It, but he still tells Marcus he doesn't have the money. Marcus gets upset, and runs him over with his car."

I chewed on her suspicion, looking for holes.

"That doesn't totally make sense. What bookie kills someone who owes him money? You're definitely not getting your money back if the person is dead. And why would Elijah ask to meet behind Cheesy Does It if he didn't want people to know about Marcus? It's not exactly a private alleyway. The patio and the bathrooms are right to the side there."

Estelle sat back in her seat, deflated. "You might be right. He wouldn't be a very smart bookie if he did all that. But why did Marcus drive all the way up here? And why has he been acting so suspicious? There's definitely something going on with him."

Estelle's phone gave a chirp in her hand. She tapped the screen, then gasped.

"What? What is it?" I strained my neck to try to see the screen. Had a murder shown up on Marcus' arrest records?

"It's a notification on my police scanner app."

"There's an app for that?"

"There's an app for everything, my dear." She tapped a couple more times on the screen. "A body was found at Holliston College this afternoon. They aren't releasing many details, though."

A body at the college? "This has to be related to Elijah's death, right? Does it say where it was found?"

She studied the phone screen. "There's an address, but I don't recognize it." Her eyes were twinkling as she looked up at me. "Let's go find out."

We hurried to the front door, falling back into our raincoats as we ran.

"Where are you going?" Miles asked from the foyer. "I was going to put on a pot roast for dinner. Simone, would you like to join?"

"Miles, dear, there's been another murder!" Estelle sounded like a fifties-era actress. "We must find our killer soon! We have no time for pot roast!"

A pot roast actually sounded pretty good just then, but I didn't think I'd be able to slow Estelle down. Plus, I wanted to see about this dead body, too. It had to be related to Elijah's death since it was on the campus he taught at. Had Marcus killed again?

"Oh, dear," Miles said, fiddling with his bow tie. "Well, I suppose I can wait to put the roast in. I was getting close to figuring out how I was bested, so maybe I should keep working on that." His voice faded as his attention turned back to the chess board. I had to laugh. These two sure had their one-track minds about certain things. Miles would likely forget about the pot roast as he spent the rest of the night replaying this chess game over and over until he got to the answer, and Estelle wouldn't give up until she found a murderer.

Estelle and I ran back outside and climbed into my car. She plugged the address into the GPS and we were off.

We drove in silence, the disembodied voice coming from Estelle's phone leading us to another dead body. Who were we going to find this time?

The GPS guided me onto the main drive of the college, and I drove towards the flashing lights and sirens. We pulled up to a stop in front of the sociology department. My stomach dropped at the thought of what we were about to see.

"This has to be related to Elijah's death, right?" I asked as we unbuckled our seatbelts and climbed out of the car.

"It must be. Two deaths in one department is not going to look good for enrollment numbers."

Yellow caution tape was strung about, and a group of people gathered near a small outdoor sitting area by the entrance to the building. Past the tape, a group of people in uniform stood over something on the ground. Students were crying in the group around us. Who had died?

Maybe if we got close enough, we could hear the police say something useful. Unfortunately, the grassy area in front of the caution tape was quickly filling up with rubberneckers, and it was getting hard to see over heads.

I turned to a young woman standing next to us. She was in overalls, her hair in space buns, crying her eyes out. She might know what had happened.

"What happened here?" I asked.

She turned her tear-stained gaze to me. "It's Professor Martell!" she cried out. "He's dead!"

Some friends of hers heard her outburst and pulled her

into their group to console her. I turned back to the scene in front of me.

Quincy was dead? What happened to him? We'd just seen him yesterday at the funeral.

"What do you think happened?" Estelle's voice was low next to me.

"I don't know."

The crowd we were in was continuing to inch closer to the crime scene, trying to get a better look at the body and what had happened. The police had set up a perimeter around his body to try to keep the crowd back, but we could just make out a pair of legs sticking out. The number of officers onsite had me convinced this wasn't an accident or death by natural causes. Someone had killed Quincy, like they'd killed Elijah.

Something clicked in my head. "Where's Patel?" I looked around the officers, but I didn't see the detective anywhere.

"What do you mean?" Estelle asked.

"She should be here, shouldn't she? Quincy's death must be related to Elijah's."

"Maybe she doesn't know about this. We're in a different jurisdiction, aren't we?"

She had a good point. The Holliston PD wasn't connected with the Pine Brook PD.

Speaking of which... "How did you learn about this?" I asked, turning away from the body and focusing on Estelle. "Your police scanner app must pick up tons of reported crimes. How did it know about this one?"

"I set it up so that I'd get alerted about any crimes in Holliston. I figured it was a good idea to see if anything else happened here. I've gotten a lot of notifications about burglaries and car break-ins over the past couple of days, but I figured a dead body was more relevant to our investigation."

What did it say about me, that I hung out with people who had police scanner apps set up to tell them when there had been a murder? I'd need to spend some time reflecting on what kind of person this made me.

"We need to tell Patel what happened." I pulled out my phone and quickly dialed the detective's number.

"What?" Her voice was curt on the other end.

"Hello, detective. Listen, I'm at Holliston College. Quincy Martell was murdered. You might want to get out here. I think it's related to Elijah's death."

A pause stretched on for so long, I worried she'd hung up the phone.

"Okay." A click, and the call ended.

I slipped my phone back into my pocket. "I think she heard me. Hopefully, she gets out here soon."

We hung around for a little while longer, watching as police officers and other police personnel dealt with the crime scene. Pictures were taken, measurements were written down, and students sobbed around us at the death of another professor.

Did Marcus kill Quincy, like he killed Elijah? Estelle's police scanner app had said that Quincy was found this afternoon, but didn't say what time. We'd been with Marcus for a couple of hours that afternoon, following him to that warehouse in Tacoma. Was it possible he'd snuck out a back door and used a different car to drive to campus and kill Quincy?

"It's possible Marcus left that warehouse through another exit, came here and killed Quincy, then came back to the warehouse and confronted us to give him an alibi,"

Estelle said, somehow reading my mind. "He has to be our killer, right?"

"Maybe. Why kill Quincy, though? Did he know something about Elijah's death?"

Estelle wrapped her arms around herself as the wind picked up. Students had started to disperse as the night wore on. Patel was nowhere to be found. Why hadn't the Holliston police called her when they realized another professor had been killed at the college? Were the two police departments not working together on Elijah's death?

"There's nothing else for us here. We should get you home." I wrapped my arms around the older woman, trying to keep her warm.

"Hopefully Miles has started that pot roast." She slid her arm around me, and we headed back to the car, scenes of murder running through our heads.

20

The inn was quiet when I pulled up. I'd dropped off Estelle at her home but had skipped the pot roast. It was getting late, and I was tired. Finding another dead body was really wearing on me. I wanted to check on Chrissy and make sure she was okay.

Entering the building, I spotted Tracy at the front desk. That was odd. Usually she went home by this time. I walked over to her.

"Why are you here so late? Don't you need to get home to your cat?" I asked her.

"I wanted to check in with you before I left," she said. "I didn't think you'd be out for so long."

"Sorry, I got caught up in some things. I was hoping to talk to Chrissy before turning in for the night. Have you seen her?"

"No, she's not here."

Drat. Her absence after another man's death was not going to look good to the police.

"Did she say where she was going?"

Tracy shook her head. "She left a while ago, said she was going out and that she'd call you. I'm guessing she didn't."

"You're right about that." I glanced at my phone, but I didn't have any missed calls or messages. Where was Chrissy going this late?

"What time did she leave?" I didn't really believe she had had anything to do with Quincy's death, but I knew Patel would ask this question, and, if I could establish Chrissy's alibi now, then I wouldn't have to worry about my sister getting arrested for something she didn't do.

"Around six o'clock," Tracy said. "She didn't say where she was going."

Well, this was not good at all. Quincy might've been killed then. Where was Chrissy?

I pressed her number on my phone and held the phone against my ear, listening to it ring. When it landed in her voicemail, I groaned and hung up, tossing my phone back into my purse.

"No answer. Where could she have gone?"

"I don't know. What's the issue? She's a grown woman, right? She probably just wanted to get away from the inn for a bit."

I didn't want to go blabbing around town about another murder, but I needed Tracy to understand the seriousness of Chrissy disappearing like this, and how it might look to the police.

I leaned in close, dropping my voice. "There's been another murder, and I'm worried what the police will think if they learn that Chrissy wasn't here tonight."

Tracy gasped. "Oh, no! Who died?"

"Another professor at the college. He was murdered this evening."

"Oh, jeez." Tracy looked down at the desk in front of her,

running her hands along the smooth wood. "Chrissy did seem pretty determined to get out of here earlier. And a few people saw her leave, too, so I couldn't just say that she was around all night."

"Oh, Tracy, you can't lie for her! That wouldn't be good."

"Simone, you need to understand something." She looked up from the desk, her face tense. "This whole situation looks bad right now. Chrissy shows up in town and runs into an ex, and then the next day she finds his dead body? And now there's another dead body, and she's nowhere to be found? Why is she even in town? Did she know he was going to be here? I can guarantee you that these are all the questions the police are asking right now."

She was right; I knew that from Patel. I didn't know what she wanted me to say, though. Chrissy was making some bad decisions, but she wasn't here to answer for herself or what she was doing.

"I know how bad things can get in a situation like this," Tracy said.

She was right. She'd dealt with something very similar in the past.

"I don't want anything to happen to your sister, but you need to get her to talk to you. She has to tell someone the truth."

"You're right, you're right, of course you're right," I said, throwing my hands up in the air in exasperation. "I just wish I knew what to do next."

"Well, I would recommend trying to get a hold of Chrissy. These murders won't be solved tonight, but you need to find her and figure out where she's been. I have to get home, but call me if anything comes up." She squeezed my hand and left me alone in the inn.

It was late and I was tired. But I couldn't stop buzzing. I

needed to know where Chrissy was. I needed to know who had killed Elijah, and now Quincy. Where could I find those answers?

I remembered who I'd last seen with Quincy. It was late, but I hoped she would talk to me. I put up the "Back Later" sign at the front desk, knowing we wouldn't have anyone stopping by until morning, and headed back outside, Kristina's number already dialed into my phone.

KRISTINA AGREED to meet at a diner in Holliston. She sounded surprised to hear from me so late at night, but didn't ask any questions.

I pulled up into the diner's parking lot thirty minutes later and spotted her through the plate-glass window sitting at a table. I parked and hurried into the diner, lifting my collar against the cold. Kristina waved when she saw me come in, and I motioned to the server for a coffee.

"Thanks for meeting with me," I said, sitting across from Kristina and accepting the coffee from the server.

I took a sip of the coffee, which was burnt, but I was too tired to complain and send it back. I needed the caffeine if I was going to get through this night.

Kristina looked much better than she had at Elijah's funeral. Her color had returned to her cheeks and her hair was shiny. I was glad to see she was handling things well. But did she know about Quincy?

"What's this about?" she asked. "Have you learned something about Elijah's death?"

"Not exactly. I'm not sure if you've heard, but Quincy was found dead earlier today at the college." I paused, letting my words sink in and watching for her reaction.

She raised her eyebrows, and her mouth dropped open. "Are you serious? What happened? Was he killed? Does this have anything to do with Elijah's death?"

"I'm not sure. The police are still investigating. It does seem pretty suspicious, though. Two professors from the same department, killed within days of each other? It's got to raise some questions."

"Why are you telling me this?" she asked after a moment, pausing to take a sip of her coffee.

"Because I believe their deaths are connected. Do you have any idea why someone would want to kill them both?"

"No clue. It doesn't make any sense. I mean, like I said at the funeral, Elijah and Quincy weren't close, and they didn't really like each other that much. I can't think of anyone who would've hated them both, though. Maybe someone from the college? Did you ever find Elijah's stalker?"

I ignored her question. I didn't feel like getting into Wanda and explaining about her fear of driving.

"Do you know who Marcus is? He's in town, claiming to know Elijah. Did Elijah ever mention anything about gambling?" Seemed better to just rip the Band-Aid off and come right out with it.

Kristina dropped her gaze and her cheeks reddened. "Yes. Elijah had a gambling problem. It started before we got married. He stopped for a while when we were together, but then it picked back up. He'd started out small, placing bets here and there, but then it ballooned into something he couldn't control. I couldn't put up with it for much longer. I wanted to start a family with him, and he was going on benders in Vegas on the weekends. I couldn't do it anymore, so I left him."

"Did you ever meet Marcus?"

She nodded. "A couple of times. At first, Elijah introduced him as a friend, but it became clear pretty quickly what he really was. Elijah was afraid of him a few times. I got the sense Marcus knew some scary people in Vegas, and Elijah worried that if he couldn't pay, then Marcus would send someone after him. Why are you asking about Marcus?"

"I ran into him earlier today. He was at Elijah's house. I followed him to a warehouse in Tacoma, but I couldn't tell what he was doing there. He threatened me, and it's possible he killed Quincy." I didn't say that by following him to Tacoma, I'd actually made an alibi for him. There was still a chance he'd snuck out the back and killed Quincy.

Something clicked in my head. "If you knew about Elijah's gambling problem, why didn't you say anything at his funeral?" I asked. "You knew I was looking into his death."

Kristina's cheeks reddened. "I'm sorry. I was so embarrassed about it. I didn't want to admit what he'd been doing. Plus, I didn't really know you. I hoped it didn't have anything to do with his death. I honestly thought Quincy had killed him. But now, with Marcus in town, and Quincy dead, it looks like I was wrong."

She didn't say anything for a moment, staring down at her coffee cup, the wheels turning in her head. Did she know something she wasn't telling me?

"Kristina, what is it? What do you know?"

"It's not much," she said. "But I do know Quincy had a gambling problem, too. He was better at hiding it than Elijah, but I bet he worked with Marcus, and maybe he wouldn't pay up, either. Maybe Marcus didn't just come to town for Elijah." She glanced down at her watch and her face turned to shock when she saw the time. "I didn't realize how late it was, I need to get going. I hope this was helpful. I want to find Elijah's killer more than anyone. Let me know how else I can help."

She sent me a tiny smile, then left the diner. I watched her go, then focused on my coffee in front of me.

Quincy also had a gambling problem? Maybe Quincy's gambling problem had gotten really bad, and Elijah threatened to tell the department. So Quincy killed him. Then Marcus showed up to collect his money and killed Quincy, too. But how did he get away from Estelle and me? Why would Elijah profit from blackmailing Quincy? Was there animosity between the two professors, and Elijah saw this as a way to get rid of Quincy from the department?

And why would Marcus kill two people who owed him money? Was there another reason why he'd want them dead? Did they know something about Marcus that could threaten his business, and that's why he'd driven all the way to Pine Brook from Las Vegas? Estelle had found an assault charge on his rap sheet, so he'd been violent in the past. Had he taken that anger too far this time?

Was it possible I was missing something? Was Patel aware of Marcus' involvement in all of this? It was my duty to make sure she knew about this dangerous man.

21

It was way past my bedtime by the time I got back to the inn after talking with Kristina. I needed to know if Patel had learned anything about Quincy's death, and tell her about Marcus, but I was half asleep by the time I walked into the lobby. I'd try to get a hold of her the next day.

I woke up later than normal and dressed quickly. I texted Patel and asked to meet, and headed downstairs to the lobby while I waited for her response.

"Look what I found in the storage room." Tracy stood at the front desk and pointed to a clock she'd set up behind the desk. "It works and everything."

A big yawn overtook me before I had a chance to respond. Tracy's eyebrows shot up her face.

"Long night?"

I nodded, rubbing at my eyes. "I was out pretty late last night."

"Don't tell me you're still running around trying to solve a murder? What happened to leaving these things to the police?"

"Hey, it's about my sister, okay? I can't just sit around and wait for the wheels of justice to take their sweet time. Sometimes, action is required!"

Tracy rolled her eyes, but I ignored her while I took a closer look at the clock, noting the design: chestnut wood with a detailed pattern around the base. It did look pretty old. Had Tracy finally found something worthy of the antiques fair?

"How old do you think it is?" I asked. "I bet the older stuff goes for more money, right?"

She shrugged. "Not sure. I'll leave that to the experts to decide. By the way, that landlord stopped by with this rental agreement while you were out yesterday."

She pulled out a sheaf of papers from under the desk and passed it across to me. I snatched it from her and flipped through the pages.

"Are you going to take the apartment?"

"I'm still not so sure about living so close to someone who works for the inn. Is that crazy?"

"Yes. I live two apartments down from Nadia. It's actually very convenient; we carpool sometimes."

I tried to reconcile this image with what I knew about the two women. "How did I not know that? How often do you carpool?"

"A few times a month. It's really not that big of a deal."

"I guess." I cocked my head to the side and studied the surface of the desk, thinking.

"I don't understand what's so weird about this," Tracy said. "Nick is great. I'm sure he's an awesome neighbor. You'll probably get way more produce delivered to your front door now. Besides, you're not going to find a better apartment in this town."

She was right, I knew she was right, yet butterflies still

fluttered in my stomach at the thought of seeing Nick every day. I did like him, though, and it would be nice to see him more often. And those flutters would go away on their own, wouldn't they?

~

PATEL FINALLY RESPONDED to my message. She agreed to meet me at the police station, but she didn't want me to come into the building. I parked a block down from the station and waited for her to come outside.

Patel came out of the station, glancing left and right before crossing the street. She always managed to look sleek, and today her thigh-high boots protected her jeans from the rain. Her piercing eyes took me in at once as she climbed into my car, and I prepared myself for the onslaught. I was pulling her away from real police work, and she wouldn't be happy about the interruption.

"What have you got?" she asked, crossing her arms and facing me.

And a good morning to you as well, I thought, but didn't say. Detective Patel never was one for pleasantries.

"What did you find out about Quincy's death at the college?" I asked.

"That's police business. I thought you had information to share with me?"

"Why weren't you at the crime scene last night? I would've thought the Holliston PD would call you."

She huffed. "I would've thought the same. Unfortunately, the Holliston police chief thinks Tate is an idiot, and didn't think it necessary to tell us there was a dead body at the college." She let out another exasperated sigh and stared out the window.

Finally, she turned back to me. "I shouldn't even be telling you any of this. You're a civilian, and this is all a police matter."

"I'm sorry I keep butting my head into your investigation. But I think I know who killed Elijah and Quincy."

I told her about visiting Elijah's house—making it seem totally normal and not at all weird, implying that Kristina had asked us to stop by and check on the plants—and running into Marcus. I told her he'd admitted to being a bookie and that he was in town to see Elijah. I told her about following him to Tacoma and learning from a source about how he'd been spotted driving through to Pine Brook from Las Vegas—I didn't think it wise to name Meredith by name, as I didn't want her to get in trouble at the DMV. I told Patel about how Marcus had caught us, making it seem like we'd done a very good job of hiding but that he'd been good about spotting us. I added what Estelle had found during her internet search.

"He must've killed Elijah, or at the very least, he's involved in some way. I don't know why a bookie would kill someone who owes him money, but maybe they got into a fight about it, and it got violent. Maybe running Elijah over with his car was the only thing Marcus could think to do."

I then explained how we'd learned about the other body, and how Marcus might've snuck away from us to kill Quincy. I added that I'd talked to Kristina the night before and that she'd admitted that Elijah had had a gambling problem, and that she was afraid of Marcus. Once done, I sat back in my seat, smiling, pleased I'd gotten it all out.

To my surprise, Patel was nodding and had pulled out her phone and started taking notes as I talked. She asked a couple of clarifying questions but mostly stared at the phone in front of her and chewed on her lower lip.

"Well? What do you think?" I asked finally, not able to take the silence.

She looked up at me, her eyes hard to read. "I'd just learned about Marcus and that he was in town. I was planning on sending some uniforms to his place to talk to him. I need to get more information out of him. Interesting that he got so upset at you. I would be, too, if I saw someone following me, but from the way you described it, he did seem threatening."

"So you agree that Elijah was caught up in gambling? Was that why Quincy was killed, too? Did he also have a gambling problem?"

Patel sputtered, shifting in her seat. "I didn't say that. All of this is off the record. I just...ugh."

She hung her head, taking some deep breaths. I kept silent, giving her a moment to work through whatever she was feeling.

Finally, she looked up, her eyes wide and full of emotion. "It's hard being a detective here. Tate questions every one of my decisions, and the other cops barely respect me. I know I look different from the people who normally make detective in this town, but I'm just as good as them, if not better at my job." Her voice was raised and filled the car.

"I know you're good at your job. I've seen it firsthand."

She took another deep breath, then let it out slowly. "I know. I don't mean to take this out on you. I shouldn't talk to you about any of this—Tate would have my hide if he knew we were out here—but it feels good to talk to you about these things. You actually listen to me, and, I must admit, you're not so bad at this sleuthing thing."

I smiled, sitting up straighter at the compliment.

"Which is not to say that you should keep getting involved in police investigations," she added quickly. "You're still a civilian. But it's hard to keep things from you when you're the only person I feel like I can talk these things through with."

"I don't want to do anything to jeopardize your job. But I can also be discreet," I added with a shrug. "If you ever want to talk about these things with me, I'm here for that. I want to get justice for Elijah and Quincy."

"I appreciate that. I think you're right about Elijah. It looks like it was a gambling problem. We're still confirming it, and obviously none of this should leave this car, but I think he had more secrets than anyone realized."

"Maybe Elijah had stopped paying Marcus what he owed, and that was why he came to town," I mused, staring out the windshield. "Though that doesn't explain why they were behind Cheesy Does It. Why would Elijah suggest someplace in Pine Brook to meet?"

"I don't know. I need to learn more about Marcus. Where was your sister last night?"

I gulped and sat back in my seat. Chrissy hadn't been around when I'd returned late last night. Did Patel still think she was involved? I wasn't going to tell her Chrissy had seen Elijah before his death, but did she already know that?

"You should get back to the inn. Go check on your sister." She opened the car door and began to climb out. "And thanks for listening to me ramble about work," she added, then slammed the door shut before I had a chance to respond.

Patel was right; I needed to talk to Chrissy. With another dead body, was she more involved than I realized? Or was she going to be the next victim?

22

Chrissy answered her door after three quick knocks. Her eyes widened in surprise when she saw it was me, then her features softened into a smile.

"I was just thinking about you. Come in, come in."

I followed her in and took a seat on her bed. "Where were you last night? Tracy said you went out for a few hours."

"Straight to the grilling, I see," she said with a laugh. "You're getting pretty good at this detective thing. You really know how to question a suspect, huh?"

"What are you talking about? I was worried about you last night."

Her smile fell and her features turned serious. "I'm sorry. I know I shouldn't joke about it. Everything's gotten so complicated recently. I'm just trying to find a way through all of this."

"Look, that's fine. Do what you need to cope. But I do need to know—where were you last night?"

"I just needed to get out of here. I felt like I'd been cooped up for days. I wanted to find some water to be near."

Ah, yes. My sister loved her water. It was one of the reasons she'd come back to California after grad school on the East Coast. She and Mark had met out there, but she decided she wanted to raise Hannah in Southern California. She'd always felt a strong attachment to the Pacific Ocean. She'd even enrolled Hannah in swimming lessons at a young age, so that the two of them could experience the ocean together.

"Unfortunately, we're pretty far from the coast right now, so I just went to the Puget Sound. It's not quite the same as the actual ocean, but it still helped calm me."

"Next time you decide to stare at a body of water for hours, please text me, okay? I was really worried about you."

"I promise." She reached out and took my hand. "Now, what's got you so freaked out?"

"Quincy's body was found yesterday at the college campus. The police are going to want to know where you were when he was killed."

"Quincy's dead?" She gaped at me, her mouth open. "But we just saw him at the funeral! What happened?"

"I don't have many details, but it's possible the same person killed Quincy and Elijah."

"Oh no!" Chrissy's hand flew over her mouth. "How awful. Why do the police think I killed him?"

"Because of your relationship with Elijah. And, knowing what I know now about your visit with Elijah before his death, they'll have even more reason to believe you did it."

She gripped both of my hands tightly, her eyes pleading. "You have to believe I didn't do this! I'm not a killer."

"I know you aren't, but you have to see how it looks for the police. I understand that it's hard to stay at the inn all day, but we can't give the police any more reason to suspect you of these murders. You need to stay here."

She nodded, taking a few deep breaths. "You're right. I'll stay here. Man, I sure did not expect my first murder investigation to lead to the police thinking I'm a killer. I always thought I'd be the hero in this story."

I reached out and patted her hand. "Well, we can't all be heroes, now, can we?" I said with a smirk.

She laughed and gently shoved me. "All right, Ms. Hero, go and find us a killer!"

BACK DOWNSTAIRS, I found Nadia at the front desk. She looked bored and like she didn't need my help, so I changed paths and began walking around the inn. Ostensibly, I was checking on rooms and guests and making sure the hallways were tidy, but really I was still processing everything I'd learned over the past few days.

The halls were quiet as I walked. Rain drummed against the windows as I passed them, and my feet sank into the lush carpet, muffling any sound. I picked up a dropped towel and a lost pair of sunglasses I found in the halls, and kept walking.

I was back to square one. I wanted the killer to be Marcus so badly. His reasons for being in town were suspicious, and the two people who owed him money were now dead. It made so much sense in my head. But wanting him to be the killer and him actually being the killer were two different things.

What about the other suspects? Wanda's fear of driving struck her from the list; unless she talked someone else into doing the driving, she wasn't likely to be the killer. Of course, I'd only been told about this fear; I hadn't seen it myself. Was it possible she was lying?

What about Kristina? Spouses were likely suspects, but they still needed motive. According to Kristina, she and Elijah were reconciling. Was she lying? She claimed that her car had been seen on a bridge during the window that Elijah was killed—even if she was lying about them reconciling, she couldn't have made it back to Pine Brook in time to kill him.

I finished my loop of the inn and stuck the dropped towel in the laundry room. Back at the front desk, I slipped the sunglasses into the lost and found box. The lobby was quiet, Nadia still managing things at the front desk, so I took a seat in one of the armchairs by the fireplace and stared into the depths of the fire, my thoughts spinning.

I still had so many questions and no clue about where to get answers. What I needed was evidence, something concrete I could bring to Patel to help her solve the case. But where was I going to find evidence? I'd already gone to Elijah's apartment and wasn't willing to break the law by breaking into a dead man's home.

I sat up in the armchair as something pinged in my brain. There was one place that might hold more evidence: Elijah's office. I hadn't been able to snoop around the first time I went to the college because I'd run into Quincy. What if there was something in Elijah's office that would point to the killer?

I checked the time on my watch; too late to go to the campus now, but if I left early in the morning, I might be able to get there before someone from the department came to watch the front desk. I sent a quick text to Estelle, asking her to join me. I didn't feel like snooping alone, and she'd get mad if she knew I left her out of this.

23

"Thanks for agreeing to meet so early." The next morning, I looked over at Estelle, who was bundled up in several layers. I switched on the heat in the car.

"I'm always up this early. I don't think I've ever sleuthed this early before, though. It's quite exciting."

Miles had sent Estelle into the car with a bag of cookies, and we munched on the warm chocolate chip cookies as I drove.

"How is Chrissy doing? Did you tell her about Quincy's death?"

"I did. She's still grappling with what happened to Elijah. What have you been up to? Have you found out anything on your own?"

"I have been asking around. Miriam at the station shared some more information with me. Quincy was hit over the head with a pipe, and it's possible the killer was shorter than him. The police can't say for certain until they share the evidence with a forensics specialist in Seattle, but apparently one of the officers had just taken a course on forensics and was able to point out the marks on Quincy's head that indicates the hit came from down below."

I chewed over this information, thinking about what I knew from forensics TV shows.

"But is it possible the killer could still be taller than him but angling the pipe in a certain way?"

Estelle shrugged. "That's possible, and apparently the cops acknowledged that. They're waiting until the forensics specialist can come in and take a look, but Miriam was so excited by the news, she had to share it with me."

"How did Miriam learn all of this if the case is with the Holliston PD? It seemed like they weren't sharing much with the Pine Brook police."

"Miriam has connections over there, too. Plus, Patel went and made a stink about being out of the loop on a murder that might be connected to one of her cases, and the Holliston police started sharing more information."

Patel had been upset that she hadn't known about Quincy's death first. It was good that she was now getting the information she needed to do her job.

"It's interesting that Elijah was run over by a car and Quincy may have been taken down by someone shorter than him," Estelle said. "We shouldn't assume the killer is a man."

"I agree, but I worry this just makes it look like Chrissy is the killer. She doesn't have a good alibi for the murders and she had motive. Who else could have done it? Kristina was driving over a bridge."

"Or so she says. I don't buy it. There are ways to fake that kind of thing, you know. And what about Wanda? She seemed obsessed with Elijah. Maybe Quincy found out what she had done and confronted her, so she hit him over the head. Who knows for sure whether she can drive a car?"

I nodded, thinking this over. "You might be right. I just wish we knew what the police were doing right now. I want to keep Chrissy safe, but it's hard to do when I don't know how close they are to pinning this on her. Hopefully, we can find a useful clue at Elijah's office."

The campus was still as we pulled up. I was right that things were quieter this early in the morning, which hopefully meant we wouldn't run into anyone. I parked in front of the sociology department, and we headed inside. I averted my gaze as we passed the spot where Quincy was killed, though I noticed Estelle couldn't take her eyes off of it. I hustled her inside, hoping no one would notice how interested this little old lady was in the crime scene.

Inside, things were quiet. Fortunately, no one was at the front desk, like I'd hoped. I led Estelle down the hallway towards the professors' offices, wondering if we'd know which one was Elijah's.

I paused in the hallway, staring at the form standing in the hallway a couple of doors down. My guess was that Elijah's office was the one Wanda was currently trying to break into. I cleared my throat and she jumped, dropping a bunch of tools to the ground.

"What are you doing here?" I asked, approaching her and crossing my arms, trying to look serious and official.

Wanda jumped again and gave a little squeak as she realized how close we were to her.

"I'm not doing anything," she said, putting her hands behind her back and her back to the door. "What are you doing here?"

"We're investigating a crime," Estelle said, poking her nose into things. "And it looks like you're trying to break into this office. That seems pretty suspicious."

"I'm also trying to solve a crime. And I know that you

two have been hanging around here quite a bit. That seems very suspicious, indeed."

I glanced over her shoulder. "Are you breaking into Elijah's office? What are you looking for in there?"

I didn't say that we'd also come here to break into his office—she didn't need to know about that.

"I'm a student here. I'm checking up on my professor's office," Wanda snapped back. "What are you doing here? I know your sister is a suspect in Elijah's murder. Are you here to get rid of any evidence that she did it?"

I rolled my eyes, holding back a smart remark. I had to remember that this was a young student who was probably scared because her professor was dead.

"We know you were stalking Elijah," Estelle burst out, apparently not agreeing that Wanda was some poor, innocent waif, and going for the jugular instead. "You must be here getting rid of evidence that you killed him because he wouldn't return your feelings!"

At that, Wanda burst into tears, great sobs racking her small body. Estelle and I exchanged a glance, unsure about what to do with this situation. I reached out and patted Wanda on the shoulder. We hadn't meant to make her cry, and now I felt pretty bad for arguing with her in the first place.

"I don't know what to do!" she said finally. "I know the police think I'm the killer. The one night I don't go out with my roommate, and the professor I love turns up dead. Of course they would think it's me! I've been trying to find his killer so I won't get arrested. Do you think they'll arrest me?"

"I don't know," I said honestly. Estelle and I had been pretty convinced she might have something to do with these murders at one point, so I wouldn't be surprised if the police felt the same way. But her tears looked genuine, and I didn't know what to do with that information.

"What have you found out so far?" Estelle asked, leading Wanda over to a small bench and sitting us all down. "Who do you think killed Elijah and Quincy?"

Wanda shrugged. "I haven't found out much. I do think the professors might have been doing something illegal. I found some notes in Professor Martell's office that make me think he was getting into something he shouldn't. But I couldn't really tell what they were, and I didn't want to bring it to the police in case they got mad at me for breaking into his office."

"Yeah, maybe don't tell them about breaking in," I said with a grimace. "What did the notes say? What makes you think they were suspicious?"

"Well, I'm not really sure, but they were slips of paper with numbers and names on them. I googled some of the names, and it looks like they matched up with horse races in the area. I guess betting isn't exactly illegal, but Professor Martell had them crumbled up like he didn't want anyone to see them. And then I remembered seeing something in Professor Norris' office with the same handwriting on it, so I wanted to check in his office to see if he'd been to the same place with Professor Martell." She dropped her head into her hands, giving it a shake. "But I just can't believe Professor Norris would get into something like that! He was always so kind to me. Do you think it's really true?"

It had been confirmed from multiple people that both professors had a history of gambling, which would explain the notes Wanda had found in their offices. While I had thought Elijah seemed nice enough when we met, it could've been possible that he had gotten into some bad habits that were following him around. Was that what had killed him?

"Look, I don't really know what the answer is here," I said, turning back to Wanda. "We're still trying to figure out exactly what they were doing."

"There's something else," Wanda said. "I've been thinking over my last conversations with the two of them, trying to remember anything that might be helpful."

"Yes...and?" I asked after a moment when she didn't say anything.

"I wasn't sure if it was important, but then I was thinking about it more, and I realized it must be. The week before Professor Norris was killed, I heard him on the phone with someone. I'd come by to try to talk to him—this was after he stopped returning my messages, and I thought maybe if we got face-to-face, I could get him to listen to me.

"His door wasn't shut all the way, but when I poked my head into his office, he was facing away from the entrance, talking on the phone. He sounded...tense. And nervous. I probably should've just left, but I still really wanted to talk to him...so I stayed and listened. I know I shouldn't have, but I wanted to know what was going on with him."

Estelle and I exchanged a glance, but we didn't say anything about her eavesdropping.

"I heard him talking to someone about some numbers, and then he said he didn't want that person to come to Holliston. He said he'd get the money to him, but it was clear the other person didn't believe him. He sounded really scared. I still don't know exactly what they were talking about, but he did say the name Marcus at one point. Then he hung up the phone quickly, and I left before he saw me. I didn't think he'd appreciate me spying on him. And then he was dead the next week."

She burst into tears again, and this time Estelle and I both patted her back, trying to comfort her as she worked through her emotions.

Marcus must've called Elijah last week about the money he owed, and when Elijah didn't pay up, Marcus decided to drive to Holliston and collect in person. Maybe Elijah had agreed to meet Marcus behind Cheesy Does It to pay him back, but when Elijah showed up without any money, Marcus got into his car and ran him over. Of course, why would Elijah show up if he didn't have the money?

Was it possible Elijah paid him, and then Marcus ran him over for some other reason? If so, why was Marcus still in town? He needed to collect money from Quincy still; was it possible he got his money from Quincy, too, and then also killed him? That didn't make much sense. A bookie doesn't go around killing people who've just given him money. As much as Marcus creeped me out, I still had trouble thinking of a good reason for why he'd kill the two professors.

"I think you should stop snooping around," I said to Wanda once she stopped crying. Estelle handed her a tissue. "There's a real killer out there who won't be happy to see what you're doing right now. You need to be careful and let the police handle this." I was being hypocritical, but I couldn't let this poor girl get hurt because she was sticking her nose into things.

Wanda nodded, chagrined. "You're right. I promise I'll stay out of it. Can I go now?"

I nodded and she stood, glancing quickly at Estelle, then scurrying out of the department, gripping her backpack and lock-picking tools. Estelle and I watched her go, both silent.

"Do you think she'll listen to you?" Estelle finally asked.

I shook my head. "Not a chance. She's tenacious and determined. She'll probably wait a day, then keep looking around. Which means we need to do what we can to find this killer before someone else gets hurt. Maybe the Holliston police know something. Do you have any family members who work there?"

It was a long-shot, but Estelle had surprised me before.

Estelle laughed. "Honey, I only have so many family members. I'm not going to be able to help with this one."

I sat back, determined to get to the bottom of these murders but feeling more confused than ever. I didn't think Wanda was the murderer, but if not her, then who?

I PULLED to a stop in front of Estelle's home and switched off the engine.

"I thought you needed to go back to the inn," Estelle said, pulling off her seatbelt.

"Let's go inside for a bit. I need to talk to you about something."

I followed her into her home and we went into the living room, the bag of cookies from Miles still clutched in my hands. We settled down and I passed her a cookie.

"I've been thinking about Marcus," I said slowly. "I'm certain he's our killer—he's the only suspect that makes sense at this point. He has a history of violence, his reasons for being in town are shady, and he was doing illegal things with both murder victims in the past. I think we need to find some serious evidence against him to bring to the police. It's not possible he's hidden everything."

"I think you're right," Estelle said with a nod.

I let out a breath I didn't realize I'd been holding. I wasn't sure if she would agree with me, but I was glad to see we were on the same page with this. I was desperate to find another suspect for the police that wasn't my sister.

"What do you propose we do?" she asked.

I leaned forward in my seat, warming up to the topic. "I've been thinking. We need to get a hold of him. Get him to admit what he did. If we can get him to say anything incriminating, we can go to the police and tell them what we learned."

"How are we supposed to get a hold of him? We don't even know where he's staying, or if he's even still in town."

"I'm sure he's still in town." He had to be, or else my plan wouldn't work. "Is there a way to look up someone's phone number online?"

"Maybe," Estelle said thoughtfully, cocking her head to the side. "Give me a moment."

She hurried out of the room and came back a moment later with a laptop that resembled a brick. I smirked as she settled back on the couch and began typing on the keyboard.

A few moments later, she handed me a scrap of paper. "Found it!" she cried out. "Are you going to call it?"

"Not a chance," I said, typing the number into my phone. "I'm going to send him a message."

Estelle sat next to me and looked over my shoulder while I typed it out.

I know what you did. Meet me at Cuppa Joe's in one hour or I tell the police. Come alone.

I hit send and set my phone down to wait for a response.

"Oh, I just got a chill reading that," Estelle said. "You are a stone-cold detective."

I smiled, flattered at the compliment, and tried to ignore the shaking in my hands. Baseless threats were harder to deliver than I thought.

My phone dinged on the table and I pulled up the message.

I'll be there.

"Wow, maybe he really is the killer," Estelle said, reading the message. "Why would he agree to meet if he wasn't guilty?"

She had to be right. We were finally going to find Elijah's killer!

24

We decided to go to Cuppa Joe's together. At first, we planned for just me to meet with Marcus, while Estelle hung around at another table to see what happened. But we decided it would be too easy for him to threaten just one of us. If we were both there, he'd have no choice but to admit what he did.

Marcus looked as threatening as ever as he entered Cuppa Joe's, but he kept a smile on his face as he approached us.

"Ladies, what's this all about? I don't like getting interrupted while I'm watching my shows."

I gulped and looked over at Estelle, who looked as nervous as I felt. I'd placed my phone on the table in front of us and had an app recording us in case he said anything incriminating, though an app wouldn't stop him from stabbing us.

"We have some questions for you." I put on my best professional voice and tried to sit up a little taller.

I was reassured by all the people around us, but I also knew Marcus could shoot us before anyone would notice a thing. Fortunately, he took off his long trench coat, and I was pleased to see there weren't any guns on him. At least, none that I could see.

"What are you doing here in town?" I asked.

"That's none of your business." He leered at us.

"Did you kill Elijah Norris? What about Quincy Martell?"

"No, I did not kill those men. I heard about Quincy's death on the radio. It happened yesterday afternoon, right? As I remember it, you two were following me around then, so how exactly did I do it? Besides, I'm a bookie; if I kill the people who owe me money, I'm never getting that money back."

"Maybe there was a fight, and you killed Elijah because he attacked you. Then Quincy found out what you did, and you had to kill him to keep him quiet. We know exactly what happened here." I sat back, satisfied.

"You're grasping at straws," Marcus said. "You have no idea what you're dealing with."

"If you didn't kill anyone, then why are you still here?" I asked. "Why haven't you left yet if you aren't going to get your money?"

Marcus had been keeping things under control, a smile on his face, but at my words, his mask dropped and a sneer emerged. "Listen, I will not have you running around telling people I'm a killer. You two need to stay out of things you don't understand, or else grandma over here will learn how violent I truly am." He sent a threatening look towards Estelle, then stood and stalked out of the coffee shop.

I glanced over at Estelle, who was shaking in her seat, and I pulled her into a hug.

"I'm so sorry." I rocked her and wrapped my arms tighter

around her, trying to still her shaking. "You were right; I shouldn't have brought us here. I won't let him hurt you."

She nodded, but her eyes told me she was still scared. I glanced back at the door, which Marcus had just left through. Had I just put my best friend in the crosshairs of a killer?

ESTELLE and I drove in silence. I glanced over at her a few times, but she was staring out the window. I could tell she was still upset about what had happened, but was trying to keep on a brave face.

Marcus' outburst was shocking. If he was willing to threaten someone like that, especially someone as gentle and kind as Estelle, then he must've been willing to murder a man. I didn't know how he did it, but he had to be the killer.

I pulled up in front of Estelle's home and turned off the engine, but she didn't move. She was still staring out the window, though I didn't think her eyes were actually watching the world out there. She was more likely reliving what had just happened.

"Estelle? We're here. Do you need some help getting to the door?"

I hopped out of my seat and hurried over to her side, pulling open the door and grabbing her arm. She smiled and let me help her down from the seat.

"Thanks, dear, though it's not really necessary."

We shuffled up the walkway to her front door and climbed the steps together.

"My mind is a little distracted right now. I didn't expect him to act like that."

"I'm sorry for even bringing you. I didn't realize he would act like that either. This is all my fault."

Estelle turned on me, her eyes wide. "Simone, don't say that! You can't blame yourself for that man's actions. You're just trying to do something good for your sister. Besides, this is all just a part of amateur sleuthing. I can handle it."

She smiled and unlocked her front door, waving goodbye and shutting it behind her as she stepped in.

I climbed down from the porch stairs, hearing her start to move around in the small house. She looked upset, and I didn't know what to do about it. No matter what she said, it was my fault for bringing her there. I shouldn't have brought anyone with me, knowing that Marcus might've been the killer. This was all getting so dangerous.

Estelle lived just off the downtown area of Pine Brook, and I could see the main town square and people milling about. The sun had come out, and, while it was still cold, people were braving the weather to get some sun.

All I had back for me at the Hemlock Inn was a sister who wouldn't be honest with me and guests wondering where they could get more towels. Tracy probably expected me back soon, but I wasn't ready to turn in just yet. I needed some time alone to think.

I crossed the street and made my way downtown. Estelle's street led right to the main drag, just around the town square. People were sitting in the grass, perched on park benches, and strolling down the sidewalks, window shopping or grabbing a bite to eat.

Cheesy Does It still looked busy and clearly wasn't suffering for having a dead body on the premises just a few days before. I knew very well, from my experiences last month, that a dead body was likely to bring more guests than you knew what to do with. People had some kind of morbid curiosity that drove them to wanting to know more about a violent death. It was partially why I kept getting caught up in murder investigations, too.

I strolled down the sidewalk, nodding hello to the townspeople I recognized. Cars zoomed up and down the street, reminding me that it was nearing the end of the day and people were heading home from work. I knew I should get back to the inn soon, but I needed some time away from everything.

Why did I keep thinking I could solve these murder cases? All it led to was unanswered questions and the people around me getting hurt. I was trying to save my sister, but I didn't even know if she wanted my help, from the way she wouldn't tell me things. I couldn't seem to stop myself from getting involved in these cases. One day, it might actually get me killed, if I wasn't careful.

"Simone!" Abby called to me from the other side of the street. She glanced both ways, then jaywalked across the street. Abby owned a clothing store in town, and we'd been friendly since I'd moved to Pine Brook.

"I thought that was you." She pulled me into a hug, smelling like lavender and denim. "Doing a little shopping?"

"Not really." I glanced down at her outfit: bootcut jeans and peasant tunic, much chicer than anything I could pull off. "Love the top. Branching out at the shop?"

"Oh, you like?" She did a pose for me and I couldn't help laughing. "I thought it might be a little edgy for Pine Brook, but this town could use some fashion sense. I've priced them low at the shop, so hopefully people will be willing to take the risk and try something new. I'm actually heading back there now, care to join me?"

She looped her arm through mine and we set off down the street.

"I heard you've been apartment shopping. How's that going?"

"Pretty good. I think I found the perfect one."

"Oh, that's amazing!" Abby gave a squeal and clapped her hands together. "I'm sure you'll love it."

We chatted a bit more, coming to a stop at a crosswalk. We waited for the light to turn green.

Abby was right, that apartment was going to be great. I'd forgotten how perfect it had been when I'd toured it, given how much investigating I'd been doing recently, but I was glad I was going to take it. If things got awkward between me and Nick, well, Pine Brook had lots of produce sellers, didn't it?

The light at the crosswalk was still red when I felt a hand against my back. I tensed at the pressure, thinking someone was trying to step around me. But then, before I realized what was happening, I was in the street, stumbling over the curb and dropping to my knees. Heart racing, I glanced up to a car barreling down in my direction, screams coming from the crowd behind me.

25

The car's tires squealed as its driver hit the brakes. Hands grabbed at my shoulders and arms, and, as quickly as it happened, I was pulled out of the street, back onto the safety of the sidewalk.

I took a few deep breaths, my heart pounding as I stared out at the road in front of me. Several people were holding me up, and Abby broke through the crowd to get to my side, grabbing my arms and pulling me close for a tight hug. I pressed my face against her shoulder, inhaling lavender and denim, as waves of terror coursed through my body. What had just happened?

"Are you okay?" Abby asked, pulling away from the hug as the people behind me settled me on the sidewalk.

I murmured my thanks to them. My legs were unsteady but Abby gripped my side, helping me stand. Her eyes scanned my body, checking for injury.

"I'm okay," I said, surprised to hear my voice come out normal. Didn't it know I'd almost been killed? "Did you see what happened?"

Abby shook her head. "No idea. One minute, we were

talking about the apartment, and the next you were gone. I didn't even realize you'd stepped into the street until someone screamed."

"I didn't step into the street. I was pushed."

I looked around the crowd, trying to figure out where the person who had done this had gone, but there were too many people around and no one looked suspicious. People mostly looked scared, staring at me from a distance with wide eyes.

"Oh, Simone, are you okay? I just saw everything!" Vivian, the realtor from the first apartments I'd looked at, came up to us, concern written all over her face.

"I'm all right," I said, hysteria still in my voice.

Adrenaline was leaving my body, and my muscles started to stiffen. This was going to hurt in the morning.

"I'm just a little freaked out. Did you see who did it?"

"Did what?" Vivian asked, glancing between Abby and me. "I thought you stumbled into the street? These sidewalks can be so bumpy sometimes. Last month, Arthur MacMillan slipped on his walker and almost landed in the street. The town council keeps promising they'll pave them over, but nothing ever happens. I'll help you write a complaint letter to them if you'd like," she added with encouragement, as if a complaint letter was going to solve the fact that someone had just tried to kill me.

"That's okay, I don't need to do that."

It was getting late, and I wanted to get back to the inn and out of the street. I didn't know if the person who pushed me was still around, but I felt like a sitting duck just standing here.

"I actually should get going. Thanks for helping."

"Are you sure you don't need a doctor?" Abby asked as I

turned away, but I waved her off. I wanted to get back to the safety of the inn as soon as I could.

I headed back to my car. Clouds had started rolling in and the bucolic town square looked more ominous now. Was the person who pushed me still out there? Or had they fled as soon as they realized I wasn't hurt? Who had done this?

Was it Elijah's killer? Did they suspect I was getting too close to the truth and I needed to be silenced? My thoughts flashed to Marcus. He'd just been with Estelle and me, and easily could've followed me back to the town square. Had he decided I knew too much and needed to get rid of me?

Back at my car, I climbed in, never once taking my eyes off my surroundings. I wanted to get back to the inn, where I was safe from killers, but I paused with my key in the ignition. Things were getting too intense by the minute. I thought I had a handle on things, but clearly Marcus was getting more and more dangerous. I needed to tell the police what had happened. I turned on the engine and pointed my car in the direction of the police station. Patel needed to know what was going on.

I CALLED Patel as I drove to the police station. At first, she didn't answer, and I had to dial again before she finally picked up. She sounded annoyed to hear from me, but something in my voice must've convinced her to listen to me.

"Meet me at the police station, but go around the back. Tate's hanging around the front, and I don't want him to see you."

I made it to the station quickly and parked in the back

parking lot, near the police cruisers. Clouds had rolled in as I drove, and I wrapped my jacket tighter around myself as I left my car.

Patel met me at the back door of the station, her mouth set in a grim line.

"Come in," she said, holding the door open for me.

I followed her inside, through the maze of cubicles, offices, and storage areas in the back of the station. Some police officers milled around, talking on phones or to each other, or filing paperwork, but no one really paid us any attention.

I got the sense that Patel mostly worked under the radar at this station unless she was bringing in a killer. She was the silent type, and the people around her seemed to expect that from her.

She led me back to her desk, which was piled high with papers. We took a seat, and she looked around to make sure no one was going to interrupt us.

"What's going on?" Her face didn't betray her emotions and I hoped she wouldn't be upset with me for what I was about to say.

I took a deep breath and explained everything that had happened since we last talked, starting with confronting Marcus and his threat against Estelle, and getting pushed into the street. I told her that it was still possible for Marcus to have killed Elijah and Quincy, even if he was claiming he hadn't done anything. Patel listened, her face blank.

I sat back once I finished, tense as I waited for her response.

Her mind continued moving as she processed what I said, and she looked off to the side as she thought. Then she pulled out her phone and typed some notes into it, not looking up at me as she did. I guess she didn't need to confirm anything I said.

Finally, she put her phone away. "You really shouldn't be doing this. I can't believe you brought Estelle with you to confront a suspect. I can't even believe you decided to confront a suspect! You're not a police officer, and you're going to get someone hurt."

At least she wasn't saying anything I didn't already know.

"I know you're right. I know I messed up. I didn't think Marcus would do anything while we were in public. But you have to admit, it does make him seem that much more suspicious, right? And what about the person who pushed me? He easily could've followed us back and seen that I'd gone walking off on my own."

"Did anyone see what happened? Can anyone say if he was around?"

I sat back in my seat, deflated. That was the only information I didn't have.

"No. No one said they saw anything. That realtor I told you about, Vivian, came up to me and said she saw what happened, but she thought I slipped. No one knew that I was pushed."

"And you're sure you were pushed?"

Patel looked up at me with innocence in her eyes, as if asking a perfectly normal question, but I could tell that she was also trying to detect if there was any way I was wrong about what happened.

I nodded firmly. "Yes. I know what happened out there. I know how it sounds, but someone put their hand on my back and pushed me. I didn't see anything, but I know what I felt."

I'd gone back and forth myself, questioning if I had in fact felt that hand, or if I'd somehow stumbled. But I'd been standing a few inches back from the edge of the curb, and we'd been preparing to step forward and keep walking once the light turned, so I knew that I wasn't moving before that point. And, I'd felt a hand. I couldn't describe the hand, but I knew it was back there.

"Is it possible someone bumped into you? Maybe they were coming from the other side, and they stumbled and bumped into you, knocking you down."

Patel seemed determined to explain this away, but I was confident that I knew what happened.

"I know it's hard to believe because we want to think that Pine Brook is safe, but I know what I felt. They didn't just bump into me. There was a hand on my back. I think someone doesn't want me snooping around anymore. And they've decided this is the best way to get me to stop."

"While I don't like their methods, I have to agree with them." Patel sat back in her seat, her mouth grim. "You're making someone very angry. You're putting yourself and others in danger by asking these questions. You need to leave this to the police."

"I try to do that, but you don't have the resources to solve this thing. Are the Holliston police even trying? I found Elijah's body, and no one from their force has come by to talk to me. It feels like I'm the only one looking for this killer. Except you, of course," I added hurriedly.

Patel sighed. "The Holliston PD is dealing with a string of burglaries in one of their richer neighborhoods, and the homeowners in that neighborhood are up in arms about what's going on. They're already short-staffed, and since Elijah was found in Pine Brook, they don't have any issues with fobbing him off on us. Unfortunately, I don't have the support here to keep things moving fast enough. Tate is all over me to get this thing solved, but won't give me the manpower to actually canvass and find anyone who might know anything about what's happening."

"Clearly, the killer thinks I'm involved in this, and my life is now at risk. I can help you find them if you just tell me what you know. I know I'm a civilian and that this goes against department policy, but please. My life is at stake now."

Patel studied me, seemingly grappling with her personal honor code inside. She'd already told me she struggled to talk these things through with the other cops at the department. While it was true that my life was now at risk, I hoped that a small guilt trip could convince her to share more with me.

She leaned forward, dropping her voice. "None of this leaves this room. We'll both face charges if it gets out what I'm about to tell you. No telling your sister, no telling Estelle, no telling anyone. Got it?"

"Got it." I held back a smile as I waited for her to share.

"We confirmed Kristina's license plate was tagged by the toll bridge when Elijah was killed, and she's been cooperating fully with our investigation. I've been looking into Marcus, but I can't find much information on him. One of my officers is digging into his past in Las Vegas, but like I said, I don't really have the manpower for a full hunt right now. I'm just trying to keep my head above water. We did manage to pull Elijah's phone records."

She shuffled through some papers on her desk, pulling out a folder and flipping it open.

"The only calls he made in the days leading up to his death were to a cousin in Florida and a lawyer in Seattle. He received a couple incoming calls from Marcus, but the records don't show any outgoing calls to the same number. We're speculating that that was Marcus trying to get a hold of him about his unpaid debt, before deciding to drive up here and collect in person. We spoke with Elijah's cousin, who said they talked a couple times a year on birthdays, but he didn't know anything about why Elijah was killed. We're trying to get the lawyer to tell us what they were talking about, but attorney-client privilege is making that a challenge."

I sat back in my seat. Did these calls hold the answer to his death? Or were they simply the kinds of calls anyone would make?

Wait a second—why weren't there any calls from Chrissy? Oh, right—she'd said they'd used Facebook to message back and forth. Those messages wouldn't show up on his cell phone records, which meant Patel had less evidence that Chrissy was involved.

"What's happening back here?" Chief Tate stomped toward us, nostrils flaring.

Patel stood, and I quickly followed, trying to shrink down in front of Tate. He was the last person I wanted to see right now.

"Simone was answering a few questions for me," Patel said. "She thought she had some more information to share about what happened, and we were just going over everything."

"Is that so?" Tate studied me, as if trying to detect the lie. "I thought her sister was your number one suspect? Seems a little inappropriate for her to be here while we're building a case against her sister."

I tried to keep my face straight, but inside I was stressing out. Chrissy was still their main suspect? Patel hadn't said anything about that.

Patel grimaced. "I haven't narrowed in on any one suspect. Not all alibis have been confirmed yet. I'm keeping all of my options open right now. If you have any issues with my detective skills, you can direct those to me." Patel stood up to him, and I was proud to see her strength.

"Well, her sister still seems like the best choice. Ms. Evans here better stay away from this station if she doesn't want anything to happen to her sister." Tate sneered at me, then left.

"Sorry about that," Patel said. "You know how he gets sometimes. I think it's probably best if you left now."

I agreed, and thanked her for talking to me. She led me out of the station to the back parking lot, which was now covered in rain. Drat. The rainstorm had started.

I tried to ignore Tate's voice in my head as I drove away from the station. Was he really going to arrest Chrissy? I needed to get back to the inn and make sure she was okay.

26

I went back to the inn, desperately needing to talk to Chrissy. I was still shaken from getting pushed into the street and, after talking with Patel and learning that Tate was convinced Chrissy was the killer, I needed to know what else my sister was keeping from me. Maybe she knew more than she realized.

I found Chrissy right away in the lobby of the inn. She sat in front of the fireplace, reading a book she must've found on one of the bookshelves nearby. Her face was clean and her hair pulled up into a bun, and she was wearing a thick sweater and dark jeans. She glanced up with red and puffy eyes, and I knew she'd been crying recently.

"Is everything okay?" I asked, coming to sit next to her. Clearly it wasn't.

"Oh, this," she said with a laugh, gesturing to her face and not looking me in the eye. "No big deal. Just a lot of stress the past few days. I talked to Hannah earlier, and she's wondering when I'm going to come home. I think it might be time to start figuring out when that is going to happen."

A knot of unease took shape in my stomach. I understood the desire to want to leave and be with her daughter, to escape everything that was happening right now. I'd felt that way when I was involved in a murder investigation last month. Still, with what I'd just heard from Tate, leaving might look more suspicious.

"I'm not so sure if that's a good idea. I know Patel wants you to stay in town in case she has any more questions for you. I think they're getting close to arresting someone for Elijah's death, and she's not going to take it as a good sign if you leave now."

Chrissy flapped her hand, as if flapping away my concerns, not bothered by some small-town detective.

"I get that it doesn't look great, but I'm sure it wouldn't be that big of a deal. Besides, I need to be with my daughter. All I'm doing here is stewing in my stress and waiting for them to arrest me. I think it's best if I leave, and I can find a lawyer in L.A. to coordinate with them if they have any questions."

My brow furrowed. "A lawyer probably isn't a bad idea, but I don't understand why you can't stay for a few more days. I'm sure everything will be wrapped up soon."

"Because of my daughter, that's why," Chrissy snapped, and I raised my eyebrows at her outburst. She quickly laughed to cover it up, though the smile didn't reach her eyes.

"Sorry, I'm a little jumpy," she went on, turning her attention back to the book in her lap and fiddling with the cover. "Hannah's been having some trouble at school recently—some girls are teasing her about her hair—and I really think I need to be home with her right now. It was a mistake coming here in the first place."

That was an understatement. Of course, she couldn't have known that a man would end up dead, two men, in fact, but leaving her husband suddenly after a big fight was not the wisest choice.

Still, I understood the desire to want to be back with her kid, especially if Hannah was getting teased in school. I knew the pain of growing up with hair that looked different than all the other kids. Hannah was beautiful in my eyes, but biracial hair could be a challenge. It was important for Hannah to see her mom and her natural curls every day.

"Listen, why don't you take a day to think about this? We can go talk to Patel together in the morning. Maybe if you explain about Hannah's situation, she'll agree that it's fine for you to leave. I just don't think you should be making any of these decisions without talking to her first."

"I don't need permission to go see my daughter," she said, her annoyance rising again in her voice. "I don't really understand why you keep pushing the matter. I thought you wanted me out of your hair, anyway?"

I recoiled, taken aback, but trying not to show it on my face. Yes, I had thought those thoughts, but I hadn't realized it was so obvious to Chrissy. This whole conversation was quickly spiraling out of control, and I needed to get us back on track. I couldn't let her leave without answering some of my questions.

"You talked to Elijah before he died; did he say anything that might explain why this happened? Was he worried about something? You might have more information about his death than you realize. You should go talk to Patel and be honest with her."

"I'm not interested in cozying up to your cop buddy," Chrissy snapped. "You might think she's a perfectly fine person, but I know what happens when you talk to the police. I'm not interested in getting arrested for something I didn't do."

I sighed at her outburst. It was only a matter of time before Chrissy's obsession with true crime got in the way of her cooperating with the police. I couldn't deny that there was a shred of truth to the possibility of her getting arrested for something she hadn't done, especially because Tate had seemed so convinced of her guilt the last time I'd seen him. Still, she was being more difficult than she should.

Just then, something shifted in Chrissy's eyes, and I saw the truth. She was scared. She was scared, lashing out, and she genuinely thought that she would never see her daughter again. She would do whatever it took to get back home to Hannah, even if it meant looking like the number one suspect in a murder.

"Chrissy, I understand you're upset right now, but I really think you need to take some breaths and think this through rationally. You have to take some responsibility for your actions and come clean about what's really going on here."

"I have to be responsible?" She scoffed. "That's rich, coming from you. You can barely keep a pet alive, let alone a child. This inn is only standing because Aunt Sylvia knew what she was doing. Even Tracy thinks you're not that good at this job. Why else would she want you to move out of the suite? That's the first step to getting you out of her hair. You're bound to mess things up if they let you stay here too long, just like you did with that bartending job and that temp job at that factory. So don't come telling me how to handle my business, or my child. As if I'd take any sort of advice from you."

Her words gutted me like a cold knife. She hesitated at the hurt on full display on my face. However, rather than apologize and own up to what she had said, she shook her head and scoffed, leaving the lobby. I watched her climb the stairs in silence, my mind racing back over what she'd said.

Sisters always knew which buttons to push. I'd thought we'd gotten past this juvenile bickering, but clearly she was taking things further than I had realized. Hot tears pooled in my eyes as I remembered the look on her face when she'd told me how much of a failure I was. I'd hoped that, by coming to this inn and taking responsibility for the first time in my life, my family would realize they had underestimated me. But clearly that wasn't the case, as Chrissy had just shown me.

And here I was, trying to keep her out of jail! If she didn't want my help, then so be it. Why had I even decided to get involved with this in the first place? I wasn't a police officer, as so many people were happy to remind me, and I was just going to mess things up.

Had Chrissy seen something in Tracy's actions that I'd missed? I knew there had to be another reason why Tracy wanted me out of the suite. Was this the first step to driving me out of the business?

I sighed and patted my hands against my knees, trying to get my energy back but just wanting to curl up in a ball in my bedroom. Lola came over and gave me a lick, and I ruffled her ears in response.

"You don't think I'm a failure, do you?" I asked her, but she simply plopped down next to me on the floor and stared up at me with her puppy eyes. She wasn't much of a cheerleader.

What was I supposed to do now? There was still a killer out there, and my sister didn't want any of my help. I'd already been threatened once, almost killed by an oncoming car. Could I even stop investigating and stay safe? Or was the killer going to keep coming after me until I was dead?

27

Lola and I sat by the fire together. I stared into the flame's depths, Chrissy's words running through my head.

Was she right? Was this all a mistake? Or was she simply lashing out because everything in her life was messed up, and this was the only way she knew how to handle it?

The rational side of me, the side that had solved two murders and run an inn for a month, knew that it was the second reason. That side of me knew Chrissy's actions didn't really have anything to do with me, and that if I gave her some space and some time to calm down, she'd eventually apologize and realize she'd made a mess of things. The rational side of me knew all of that.

But the irrational side, the side that was still eight years old and amazed by her sister every single day—that side of me was crushed. That side felt like a small child again and wanted to do whatever she could to make it up to her big sister. I had to force myself to stay in front of the fire, in the open lobby, where anyone could walk in, rather than running to my room and curling in a ball and crying, or running up to Chrissy's room and begging for forgiveness. Neither of those options was very wise, and I wanted to do what I could to keep myself from regressing in that way.

Even if what Chrissy was doing didn't really have anything to do with me, it was still hard to handle her saying those things to me. I had to question everything about the decisions I'd made in the past few weeks, and wonder if I was really doing what was best for me, or if I was running from something. Chrissy had come up here because she was running away from her husband and her responsibilities; was it so much of a stretch to say that I was doing the exact same thing?

"You look like you've seen a ghost."

My head shot up, my cheeks warming. Tracy stood in front of me with her arms crossed, her hips jutted to one side, and her head cocked. When she saw my face, something shifted in hers, and she sat next to me on the couch, placing her hand over mine.

"Is everything okay?" Her voice was now serious, her expression gentle. "I was joking about the ghost. Unless you really did see something? This inn is pretty old; I wouldn't be surprised if you stumbled onto something spooky."

That raised some questions for me, but that was for another day.

"I'm okay." I sat up a little straighter and plastered a smile on my face. "It's been a long day."

Tracy studied me for a moment, cocking her head even more to the side as she interpreted my face and my words.

"It's only three o'clock. You've still got a lot of the day left to get to. Did something happen?"

Chrissy's words flashed through my head again and I dropped my gaze. How could I tell Tracy what harsh things my sister had said to me moments ago? I could barely admit them to myself.

"It's nothing. Chrissy's feeling a little defensive, and we got into an argument. No biggie." I cursed myself as a single tear rolled down my cheek, and my voice cracked on my words.

"Oh, Simone, I'm so sorry." Tracy wrapped her arms around me and pulled me into a hug, pressing my head against her shoulder. "Sisters can be so cruel."

"You have a sister?" This was news to me. Tracy didn't talk much about her personal life.

"Several. But that's not important. What exactly did she say? Did she admit to being involved in Elijah's death?"

I recoiled, horror strewn across my face. "No! Of course not!" Since when was Tracy asking questions about Elijah's death?

"Sorry," she said, holding her hands up in a placating gesture. "People talk around here. Everyone's wondering what happened, and I thought maybe she said something to you, from the way your face looked when I first showed up. What did she say to you? Clearly it was something bad enough to cause you to react like this. I haven't seen you this upset since the last time you were questioning whether you should stay and run this inn."

"Really?"

Had that really been the last time? I'd had some doubts about running the Hemlock recently, especially since Chrissy had shown up, but I hadn't realized that it had been so long since I'd truly questioned things.

Tracy nodded. "I had to talk you off a ledge last time, too. I know you think you're not very good at this, but you've made a big difference here, even in such a short amount of time. I'm happy to have you here."

"But you don't think I'm making it worse by staying around? You don't think you all would be better off if I found someone with actual experience to come run this place?" I'd had these thoughts myself over the past month, but hadn't been able to voice them. Now that Chrissy had put them into my head, I had to question whether she was right.

"Of course not!" Tracy laughed. "You think I want to deal with hiring someone new and helping them figure out how to run this place? Besides, your aunt left you this inn. She saw something in you, and she wanted to give you a chance to do something bigger than you'd been doing before. Her confidence in you is what's kept me going as we work together." Tracy paused, looking off into the distance, then focused back on me.

"Your aunt took a chance on me, too. I'd been running from something when I showed up here, and I didn't have any experience in hotel management or even customer service. Your uncle even questioned whether I was the right fit for the Hemlock Inn, but Sylvia saw something in me that convinced her I could be good at this job. And she was right—I'm great at this work. But I never would've realized it if she hadn't taken that chance on me, and if I hadn't trusted that her gut would eventually prove correct. That's what you need to do here."

I studied my hands as Tracy fell silent. I hadn't known she'd shown up to the inn without any experience, too. She was amazing at her job, so I'd assumed she'd been doing it all of her life. But clearly she also needed to learn things, and mess up, and get better. Just like I needed to do.

"You never talk about Sylvia," I said finally.

Tracy smiled and dropped her gaze. "It's hard to do sometimes. I think about her a lot. Whenever I need to make a decision, I think about what Sylvia would do. I let her presence guide my work. I know she'd be proud of both of us." She reached out for my hand again and gave it a squeeze.

Warmth washed over me as Tracy's words settled into my head, nudging out Chrissy's words for the space. I wanted to know more about Aunt Sylvia, and the partnership she and Tracy had established in creating this inn. But that could wait.

"Why have you been so eager to get me out of the suite?" The question had been on my mind ever since Tracy first suggested I find an apartment, and I had to know the truth.

"It's like I said—we'll get a lot of money out of opening the room up to guests."

"Are you sure that's it? Or is it because it's where Sylvia used to live, and you don't like the idea of me being in her space?" There, I said it. It was now in the air between us, and we'd have to deal with it.

Confusion came over Tracy's face. "Why would that matter? I'm suggesting that we let guests book the room; that means a lot of people will now be in Sylvia's space, not just you."

Good point. I hadn't thought of it like that.

"I promise this isn't personal," Tracy continued. "Sylvia wanted to move out of the suite and open it up to guests, but then she got sick. It was too hard for her to shop for an apartment, and I felt better knowing she was here, when others were usually around, in case anything happened to her. Trust me, if Sylvia were here right now, she'd agree with what I want us to do."

Relief coursed through me at her words. I'd been so convinced that Tracy wanted to kick me out, and I'd even let

Chrissy play up that insecurity in her anger. It was time I trusted Tracy and trusted my role here at the inn.

Right now, though, I still needed to figure out what was going on with Chrissy and, ultimately, who had killed Elijah. That was the question I needed to answer so things could clear up for Chrissy and she wouldn't go to jail.

Tracy and I went to the front desk. She started doing some filing while I stared out into the lobby, my thoughts all over the place.

"I still can't figure out the answer to this murder," I said. "I thought I had a good list of suspects, but it's slowly being whittled down. Marcus looks like a good option, given everything I've learned about him, but Patel isn't so sure, and I'm not going to get anywhere without her support."

I wasn't interested in getting into another situation with Marcus where I was alone with him and he was mad at me.

"What about the ex-wife?" Tracy sorted through the mail, discreetly slipping a dog treat to Lola in the process.

I shrugged. "Kristina has a pretty solid alibi for Elijah's death. Her license plate was tagged crossing a toll bridge. It's hard to argue with that."

Tracy cocked her head to the side, thinking. "Didn't you say Elijah had a stalker? That student of his? What happened to them?"

"There's no way Wanda could've done it," I said. "She doesn't drive. It's possible she's been lying about that and secretly has a license, but I doubt it. She is pretty tenacious, though. Estelle and I caught her trying to break into Elijah's office." I didn't mention that Estelle and I had gone there to do the same thing. "She's determined to find his killer."

"Have you talked to her recently? Maybe she's found a clue."

"Maybe," I said, my thoughts spinning.

Tracy turned back to her work, leaving me to my thoughts.

Maybe it wasn't such a bad idea to talk to Wanda again. What else was I going to do? Wallow because my sister knew the best way to make me question my life choices? Since when was that new?

"I think you're right," I told Tracy. "I'm going to try to find her."

I left Tracy at the front desk, figuring my best bet was to find the dorm Wanda was staying in and try to get her to talk to me.

28

Estelle came through for me again. She knew someone at the college who was able to pull Wanda's records. I again chose to ignore the fact that we were absolutely committing crimes here, and focused on Estelle as she read out the address of Wanda's dorm over the phone.

The college campus was quiet when I arrived at Wanda's dorm the next day. I hung back for a moment, watching kids go in and out of the dorm using a key card. Trying to seem normal and friendly, I followed someone into the building.

Once inside, I looked around for some kind of map of the rooms, then realized that was stupid. They don't just put the names of all the kids out in the open like that. Here, however, it did look like names were on the dorm room doors themselves, scrawled on whiteboards or masking tape. I walked up and down the hallway, looking at the doors and hoping no one would question why I was here. I found Wanda's door after two trips up and down the hallway.

"Come in!" came the response to my knocking.

Turning the knob, I stepped into the room. It was small for a two-person room. Twin beds pushed up against opposite walls, a desk behind each bed. Posters covered the walls. A girl sat at one of the desks against the far wall, and she looked up as I entered.

"What's up?" she asked, her blonde hair pulled back into a messy bun. This was not Wanda.

"I'm looking for Wanda," I said. "Do you know where she is?"

"Oh, jeez, is she in trouble?" the girl asked.

I raised my eyebrows in surprise. "No, but why would you think that?"

She sighed and crossed her arms. "She's just been acting weird lately—ever since those professors died. I'm worried about her, and I thought maybe you were the cops or social services or something."

"No, I'm, um, a friend," I said. "I'm trying to find her, though. Do you know where she might be?"

The girl shrugged. "She told me she was going to that restaurant in Pine Brook, or whatever that town is called? She said she wanted to be closer to that dead professor. Creepy, right? If you ask me, Wanda needs therapy, and soon."

She turned back to her computer, apparently done talking with me, so I left the room, shutting the door behind me.

Wanda had gone back to Cheesy Does It to be closer to Elijah? I had to agree with her roommate that it was weird. But at least now I knew where to look for her.

Wanda was where her roommate said she would be, at one of the back booths at Cheesy Does It. It looked like she'd been crying, even from this far away. Dinah and I made eye contact when I came in.

"She's been here all day," Dinah said to me, gesturing to Wanda. "She's scaring away my customers."

I sighed and watched Wanda blow her nose into a napkin, then break out into a new round of sobs. The few other patrons still in the restaurant eyed Wanda from the side, looking ready to leave.

"I'll talk to her," I told Dinah. "Maybe she'll listen to me."

"Good luck." Dinah turned back to wiping down the counter, happy to be rid of Wanda as quickly as possible.

Plastering a smile on my face, I approached Wanda's table slowly. She'd ordered a sandwich at some point, and the remnants of her meal were scattered around the table. She had a mug of what looked like coffee clutched in her hands and was staring down at a notebook on the table in front of her. Was this her sleuthing journal she'd been talking about? Was she getting close to finding Elijah's killer, and that's why she'd come back to this place?

"Hi, Wanda," I said once I was in front of her table.

Her eyes shot up and she jolted back in her seat, sloshing coffee onto the table and her hands.

"Oh, I'm so sorry." I stepped forward and grabbed a napkin for her. "I didn't mean to scare you."

"It's all right." Wanda dabbed at her hand with the napkin, not meeting my eyes, but I could still sense her watching me. "The coffee's cold."

I looked around her table, searching for some entrance into the conversation, but found nothing.

"Do you mind if I join you?" If I could sit, maybe I could come up with something to say to her.

"It's a free country." She gestured to the chair across from her. "You wouldn't guess that, looking at how the police in this town handle things, but that's what I hear."

I slid into the booth across from her and took a moment to study the young woman in front of me. She was a shell of who she'd been the first time we'd spoken. Her hair was sticking out from her head in strange patterns and she was wearing a dirty smock. Her nails were chipped like she'd been chewing on them, which she was doing now. The handwriting in the journal spread out in front of her was small and cramped, and I tilted my neck to see if I could read any of the words, but she slammed the journal shut.

"Did you need something?" Wanda looked up at me then, her eyes rimmed in red and puffy, her skin pale. What had happened to her?

I fiddled with the menu in front of me. "I was just passing through and thought I'd check in with you. Any progress on your investigation?"

"Don't call it that," she snapped. "It's not my investigation."

"I'm sorry, I take it back. Any progress on finding Elijah's killer?"

She dropped her gaze again and shuffled in her seat. "I'm stopping all that. It was a bad idea in the first place. I never should've started anything."

"What do you mean? I thought you were determined to find Elijah's killer."

She looked up at me then, fear pooling in her dark eyes. "Not anymore. Whoever did this is a very bad person, and I don't want anything to do with them."

"Wanda, what happened? What made you change your mind?"

She paused, looking up at me, then back down again. She took a deep breath before speaking again.

"They threatened my family. My parents are old and live in Florida, and somehow this person found out about them and threatened to hurt them if I didn't stop snooping around. I can't let that happen, so I'm dropping the case." She slid the notebook closer to her chest.

I glanced down at it, shocked by her revelation. This killer was now threatening elderly parents? How far would they take this?

"I see you're still looking at your notes, though. Seems like you can't really let it go?"

Wanda's face crumbled at my words, and she started sobbing again. I looked around for help, but Dinah walked back to the kitchen as soon as I made eye contact with her. I sighed and turned back to Wanda. Guess I was on my own with this one.

I reached across the table and squeezed her hand as she cried. "How did they threaten you?" I asked gently. "Did they leave you a letter or something?"

Wanda shook her head. "They left me a voicemail. The number was blocked, and they were using some kind of filter on their voice, so I couldn't even tell if they were a man or a woman. They said if I didn't stop asking questions, Barb and Richard would pay."

I assumed those were the names of her parents. I furrowed my brow as I processed her words.

"Did you tell the police about this threat?" Even though the number was blocked, maybe there was a way they could track where the call had come from.

To my surprise, Wanda shook her head. "The caller made it clear I couldn't tell the police about them. I'm not going to risk my parents on the off chance the police can actually do anything with the recording."

I sat back, deflated. Here was one opportunity to figure out who the killer was, and Wanda wasn't willing to give it to the police.

"Listen, you shouldn't even be talking to me," she said. "I know who your sister is. Don't think I haven't considered that Chrissy might be the killer. Where was she when Elijah was killed? Why is she hidden away in that inn of yours? I might be done asking questions about Elijah's death, but you and your sister still have a lot to answer for."

Her tone had taken on a malicious hint and something flashed in her eyes. This girl was upset, and scared, and would do whatever she could to keep her family safe. I could relate to that. Wasn't that exactly what I was doing with Chrissy and investigating this murder, even after being put at risk myself?

"Wanda, I promise you Chrissy had nothing to do with this." I reached out to take her hand again, but she jerked it back and hid her hands under the table. I sighed and put my hand down on the table. "I want to find Elijah's killer just as much as you do. And I was attacked by them as well."

I told her about getting pushed into traffic, and a tiny part of me was pleased to see her eyes widen and lean forward. Clearly, she was still interested in this case.

"But how do you know Chrissy wasn't the one to push you? She could've hidden in the crowd where you didn't see her."

I rolled my eyes. "Come on, it's my sister. She's not going to push me into traffic. Besides, she was back at the inn. She hadn't left in hours when I saw her. The killer is someone else, and I need to find them."

"Good luck. I'm not helping you."

I leaned forward, taking on an urgency I hadn't had before. Wanda was vital to figuring out what was happening here, even if she didn't believe she had any information to share.

"Wanda, please. You spent a lot of time with Elijah

before his death. There must be something you saw or heard that points to his killer."

She shrugged. "I told you, I don't know anything. All I remember seeing is him fighting with that woman."

My head shot up at her words. "What woman?"

"His wife. Or ex-wife, I guess?" she said with a sneer. "I told the police this already, but I overheard her and Elijah screaming at each other a couple of days before he died. The whole department did. I don't know what they were arguing about. But her alibi is so strong, I'm sure the police didn't think it was related."

I sat back in my seat. Kristina had made it seem like she and Elijah were about to get back together in the days before his death. Now Wanda was saying they'd had a massive fight?

"Look, I should go." Wanda slipped her journal into her bag and scooted out of the booth. "Good luck with everything."

She left the restaurant, but I hadn't looked away from her seat.

If Kristina had lied about them reconciling, what else might she have been lying about?

29

Back at the inn, Nadia checked in guests at the front desk and the smell of roasted chicken wafted in from the bistro. Wanda's words were seared into my brain, and I couldn't get the image of the scared girl out of my head.

"How are things with the case?" Tracy asked, coming up to the front desk with a stack of folders in her arms.

Nadia had left me alone at the front desk. I glanced around, to make sure no one was hanging around that might overhear us, and turned to Tracy. I didn't think I should share too much about what I'd learned recently, since I didn't want anything getting back to Kristina about my suspicions about her, but I thought I could tell Tracy a bit about what I'd found out.

"I don't think Wanda is the killer. She received some threats, and she was pretty scared when I talked to her about them. I can't see her faking that."

"Who do you think killed Elijah, then? That Marcus guy? Estelle said he was pretty scary."

I shrugged, still upset that I'd gotten Estelle caught up in the trouble with me. "Maybe, though Estelle and I saw him when Quincy was killed. I just wish I could confirm Chrissy's alibi. It seems crazy to me that no one saw her while she was out that morning. Maybe I should talk to more people in town to see if anyone can corroborate what she told the police. I wish I knew more about where she was that day, but she barely talks to me anymore."

"I don't know if that's the best use of your time right now. While I don't approve of you sneaking around hunting a killer, I do think you're on the right track and probably getting close. You'll better serve Chrissy if you can keep circling in on this killer."

"I wish I knew where to go from here." I paused. Could I trust Tracy? Of course I could trust her! If I couldn't trust Tracy, who else could I trust?

"I have some suspicions about Kristina," I said slowly. "She claimed she and Elijah were reconciling, but I don't think that's true. Wanda mentioned that she overheard Elijah fighting with her before his death. Kristina's supposedly got an airtight alibi, but if she lied about their relationship, maybe she's lying about her alibi, too."

Tracy thought for a moment, mulling over my words. "That does all seem pretty suspicious. Have you talked to Kristina since learning all of this?"

I shook my head. "Patel told me I should stay out of things for the time being. I don't want to step on any toes while they're building a case. Although, from the last time I talked to Patel, it seems like Tate is more determined to find evidence against my sister. That's why I think I should focus on Chrissy's alibi; if I can find someone who can place her anywhere but near Elijah, then I will worry less about his killer."

Tracy rolled her eyes. "Come on. You know you'll still

want to find his killer even if Chrissy is cleared. You're too deep in this now to give up."

She was right. I still really wanted to know who had done this to Elijah, and not just to save my sister. A man was dead, and I was there when his body was found. That wasn't something you forgot easily, and it wasn't something I could get over. It wasn't fair that Elijah was dead and his killer was still out there walking around and living life.

"Hey, you two, I've got a delivery to drop off." Nick was standing on the other side of the desk, gripping a box in his arms and smiling at the two of us. "The back door is locked and no one is answering."

My cheeks warmed as he turned his gaze on me and my palms got sweaty. Why oh why did I react this way when I saw him? It was like my body couldn't be normal around him.

"No problem," Tracy said. "Simone, do you mind helping him out? You can use the key to open the back door if it's locked." She sent me a wink that Nick didn't see, causing me to question her motives in sending me back there with him.

"At least it isn't raining," I said to Nick as we left the inn through the front door and walked around the back of the building.

We entered through the back door, and Hank hurried over to help Nick unpack. The three of us chatted for a few minutes, mainly Hank exclaiming over the gorgeous produce Nick had brought. I smiled, watching the two of them, not ready to go back to the front desk just yet. Hanging out with the two of them back here, I could pretend that things were normal.

"I've got to take care of some orders," Hank said,

glancing over his shoulder to the rest of the kitchen. "Thanks for dropping these off."

He left us then, and Nick and I looked at each other.

"Have you decided to take that apartment?" Nick asked. "I promise it's a great building, and I'm a pretty good neighbor."

Butterflies rushed into my stomach at his words, but I pushed the feelings down. This was going to be fine, right?

"Yeah, I think I'm going to take it. I really like the building and it's pretty close to the inn. I'm not interested in a long commute like I had in L.A."

"Do you think you'll ever go back?"

I shrugged. "I don't know. I'll never say never, but I'm pretty happy here. I want to help keep this inn as busy as possible. Plus, I still feel like I'm getting to know Tracy and everyone who knew my aunt."

"That's awesome," Nick said with a grin. "You're going to love the building. How's your sister doing?"

"She's okay. The police still think she's involved in this murder, though I know she didn't have anything to do with it. I'm desperate to find someone who can verify where she was on Tuesday morning when Elijah was killed. If I can just find someone, I can prove she couldn't have killed Elijah."

"Tuesday? I saw her then."

My heart stopped at his words, then it picked back up at a rapid pace. "What? Where? When?"

"Yeah, Tuesday. I was dropping off some produce at the farmer's market in town. This was around 11:00 a.m., I think. She was in line at the candle stand. I waved, but I don't think she saw me. She didn't end up buying a candle, and then she sat on a bench for half an hour, not really doing anything. I was chatting with the owner of the produce stand, and when I went to leave, I realized she was still there."

This was amazing. Nick had seen her right during the window when Elijah was killed. There was no way Chrissy could've killed Elijah before meeting me for lunch.

"How do you know for sure that it was her?"

"She was wearing this fuzzy, bright green hat. I noticed it when I saw her at the inn the next day. That's when I figured out it was your sister. I didn't realize she needed an alibi, though."

On impulse, I wrapped my arms around Nick and pulled him into a hug. I'd made fun of that green hat when Chrissy had first gotten to town. He had definitely seen her!

He hesitated for a moment, then wrapped his arms around my waist. I leaned against his body, appreciating the strength as he held me up. He also smelled delicious. These flutters weren't so bad, right? He was a good guy, and he was going to help keep my sister out of jail. These flutters just meant I liked being around him.

"I have to go," I said suddenly, pulling away as I realized how much my body was responding to being pressed up against his. "Are you willing to talk to the police about what you saw?"

"Yeah, of course. Anything I can do to help your sister."

"Amazing. Please call Detective Patel and tell her what you know. I need to go talk to someone else."

I needed to tell Chrissy what Nick had told me, even if she was still angry at me. She needed to know that she wasn't going to go to jail.

Finally, I had some good news to share with her!

~

I STOOD outside the door to Chrissy's room a few moments later, hesitating. I wanted to knock and tell her what I had learned, to reassure her that she wasn't going to get arrested now, but a part of me held back.

Was she still upset with me? Would she yell at me like she had before? I wasn't in the mood for another fighting match, and I didn't want to hear any more about how much she didn't think I could handle running this inn. I was already struggling enough with my own confidence about it; I couldn't stand it if my big sister, the person I'd looked up to for so much of my life, kept telling me how much of a failure I was.

I turned away from the door, biting my lower lip. Maybe I should just go straight to Patel? I'd gotten the impression that Tate was counting down the minutes until he could arrest Chrissy, and so maybe I should tell Patel first so that Tate wouldn't show up with an arrest warrant. But how long would it take me to get a hold of the detective again? What if Tate showed up to arrest Chrissy in the meantime, and Chrissy really believed she was being carted off to jail? Could I live with that experience for her? Could I live with my parents' anger when she inevitably told them what I had done?

No, this was silly. I sighed and turned back to her door. I was a grown-up, she was a grown-up, and we could have a civilized conversation without it turning into a brawl. She'd be thrilled to hear what I had to say, I knew she would.

I held my hand up to knock, but hesitated again. What if she wasn't thrilled? What if she thought I was wasting time and should talk to the police first? Oh, why was this so hard to figure out what to do?

Just then, Chrissy's door swung open, and I jumped at the noise. She was on the other side, peering out of the room, looking tired and like she'd been crying. She was still in her robe and wearing reading glasses. When she saw me, her face lit up and she grabbed me. My body tensed.

"Oh Simone, I'm so sorry about everything!"

It took a moment for me to realize that she was hugging me, not strangling me. The tension left my body and I wrapped my arms around her, burying my head in her neck. We stood there for a few moments in the hallway, simply being together, before pulling away and looking at each other. Chrissy was smiling, with tears in her eyes, and I was sure I looked exactly the same.

"Come in, come in," she said, stepping back into the room and gesturing me forward. "We can't have any of your guests seeing you cry in the hallway, can we?"

I followed her into her room, trying to comprehend what was happening. She wasn't mad at me? She was happy to see me?

We settled next to each other on her bed. Empty plates from the bistro were piled up on the nightstand, dirty towels lay crumpled on the chair, and her wastebasket hadn't been emptied. Had she not been allowing the cleaning staff to enter? Why hadn't I checked on her sooner?

"Simone, I'm so sorry about what I said. I was mad and upset about everything, and I just lashed out at you. But you didn't deserve any of what I said, and I'm sorry."

"I'm sorry for letting all of this get to me. I thought I was just trying to find a killer, but clearly I wasn't understanding enough of how you are handling everything, and I should've been more considerate. I want to do whatever I can to keep you safe, and maybe that meant I wasn't taking care of my sister enough."

"Oh, stop it. You did exactly what you needed to do. I've

just been a whiny baby and not being honest with you. It's time I tell you what's been going on."

Chrissy sat up straighter on the bed, clearing her throat and smoothing her hands against her legs. I reached out and grabbed her hand, squeezing it gently. She could tell me anything.

"I really did come here because Mark and I had a fight. But it was a fight about Elijah. He'd gotten in touch a few weeks ago on Facebook, wanting to see how I was doing. He mentioned that he was living in Holliston and he'd heard that you ran this place. He wanted to know if I was planning a visit up here any time soon. I told him I wasn't, but then I couldn't stop thinking about him after those messages. I wasn't planning to cheat on Mark, I swear, but I'd always considered Elijah someone who'd gotten away. I wanted to know how he was doing. I didn't even realize that he and Kristina had split up, or else I never would've come up here. I thought he was still married!

"When Mark found out we'd been chatting, he blew up at me. I didn't tell you this, but Mark's brother recently divorced his wife because she was cheating on him, and when Mark realized what I was doing, he saw red. He thought it was exactly the same, and he was worried I was going to leave him. And, of course, that's what I did. I told him I needed some time away to think, and I came up here."

"Why didn't you tell me all this? I would've understood."

Chrissy gave a sad smile. "Because I was ashamed. I knew what I was doing was wrong. Even if I didn't plan on cheating with Elijah, I was hurting Mark. He's been so busy with work for the past year or so. Hannah is great, but she needs a lot of attention, and I've been feeling unappreciated and lonely. I thought this would show Mark that I didn't need to wait around for him to have fun. I didn't think every-thing would go as wrong as it did.

"Once I got up here, I reached out to Elijah and we agreed to meet. He didn't know I'd be at the inn that morning, and I didn't realize he would be, either. When we saw each other at the bistro, it was like old times again. But then, when I saw him that night, I knew I wanted to be with Mark. I was making a mistake with my marriage by going to see Elijah. I was going to call Mark and tell him that I was sorry and that I wanted to come home, when we found Elijah's body."

I sat back on the bed, taking in everything she had said. So she had known that Elijah was here, and the fight with Mark had been bigger than she'd let on. But then she'd found Elijah's body, after seeing him for the first time in years. I couldn't imagine the kind of pain that must've been causing her. I reached for her and pulled her into another hug.

"I know the police think I killed Elijah, and I have to agree that I'm a good suspect. I'm not an idiot; I know how bad this all looks. After I saw Elijah, the next day I wanted to be alone. I actually thought about going to find some water then, but I knew we had lunch plans, so I hung around town. I don't really know what I did. All I could think about was my marriage and what a mistake I'd made.

"I wasn't honest with you about what I was doing that day because I didn't want you to know I'd been moping around town. I wasn't ready to talk about my marriage problems yet. Still, it was a mistake. I should've come back here and told you what was going on. Then at least I would've had an alibi."

My face lit up as I remembered why I'd come up here in

the first place. "But you do have an alibi! That's why I wanted to talk. You remember Nick, the produce guy?"

Chrissy waggled her eyebrows at me. "You mean your boyfriend?"

I rolled my eyes. Glad to see she still had a sense of humor in all of this.

"He's not my boyfriend. He says he saw you that day, at the Pine Brook farmer's market. He remembers you wearing this awful hat." I grabbed it from the side table and shoved it onto her head with a laugh. "There's no way you could've made it back in time to kill Elijah if he saw you there."

"Oh, that's amazing. We have to tell the police about this!"

"Nick's going there now. I think it's best if we let him go alone. We don't want the police to think we coerced him into anything." Tate was likely to think that I'd bribed Nick into saving Chrissy.

"Are you sure? What if they think he's lying, or what if they have more questions for me?"

I patted her shoulder gently. "It'll be all right. We'll let Nick talk to the police now, then I'll reach out to Patel later today and see what she thinks. You don't need to worry anymore. You're safe now."

She smiled. "You're right. It's just so crazy to think about."

"I still don't know who killed Elijah, though. I thought it was Marcus, and then I thought it was Wanda, but I don't have any proof. I have some suspicions about Kristina, but I can't figure out why she would've done it. I thought she loved Elijah. They were reconciling. Why would she kill him?"

"Oh, that's not true." Chrissy sat up. "When Elijah and I talked, he said he'd fallen out of love with her completely. It sounded like something might've happened that upset him, but I didn't ask about it."

"What? At the funeral, she told me they were reconciling."

Chrissy shook her head. "That's not what Elijah said at all. Do you think he was lying to me?"

A chill shot down my spine. I didn't think Elijah had been lying, but I was pretty sure Kristina was.

30

Chrissy began kneading her hands together, a clear sign that she was nervous. "Do you think Kristina might be involved? Has she been lying to us this whole time?"

"I'm not sure. Wanda told me she overheard Elijah fighting with Kristina before his death. I thought maybe they had made up after that fight, and that was why Kristina told me they were reconciling, but now, I'm not so sure."

"Oh, God, I can't believe she killed Elijah!"

"Let's not go that far. We still don't have all the details. We shouldn't sit here stewing—Patel needs to know what's going on."

I pulled out my phone and dialed the detective's number. No answer. Drat. I hung up and dialed again. Still no answer.

"Where is she?" Frustrated, I stood and began pacing around Chrissy's room.

"Like you said, we're not going to figure anything out sitting around like this. If Kristina is a killer, we need to find the evidence and put a stop to her."

"Where do you propose we start?" I asked. "Wanda won't talk about anything anymore, and Quincy is dead. Marcus is probably long gone by this point. We can't walk up to Kristina and accuse her of murder. We need to be smart about this."

"You're right." Chrissy thought for a moment, then noticed she was still in a robe. "And I still need to get dressed! Why don't you go back to your room and keep trying to get hold of Detective Patel? We shouldn't leave the inn, in case Kristina is out there and knows what we know. If you can't get Patel on the phone by the time I'm dressed, then let's go down to the police station together and hope they don't think we're only there to pretend that Nick's alibi is true."

"That's a good idea. Come by my room as soon as you're dressed."

I hurried out of her room and down the stairs to my suite. Once in my room, I locked the door, not wanting to make it any easier for a killer to get to me.

I kept dialing Patel as I went, but she still wasn't answering. Where was she? Did she know what was going on? Was she building some case against Kristina that we weren't aware of?

A knock came at my door. I stopped my pacing and went over, thinking that Chrissy had managed to get dressed pretty quickly. Instead, I found Kristina on the other side.

"What a surprise," I said, trying to keep my voice steady even as my heartbeat kicked up a notch. "What are you doing here?"

"I hope this is okay," she said, smiling. "I don't mean to intrude, but I've been thinking a lot about what you said, and I was hoping we could talk. Do you mind if I come in?"

I hesitated for a moment, trying to keep my face neutral.

She was carrying a purse and her raincoat in her arms was soaked. She didn't look like a threat—she couldn't be more than one hundred pounds soaking wet—but I didn't want to underestimate her. Still, I needed to keep my cool and not let on that I suspected her of murder. We'd talk briefly, then I'd get her out of here as soon as I could.

I stepped back and welcomed her into the room, shutting the door behind her. I didn't lock it this time. If she did attack me, and I started screaming, I didn't want to make it harder for anyone to break into the room.

"This is a nice suite," Kristina said, walking around the room and admiring the different furniture. "I've never been to this inn before, but it's a really lovely place."

"Thanks. My aunt tried hard to make it a nice special destination. I'm actually thinking about moving out of this suite, so we can open it up to guests. All the other rooms are smaller, and this place should attract more interest." I was rambling, but I didn't know how to act right now.

"That makes sense." Kristina took a seat on the bed. "It's so impressive that you're running an entire inn. You're an impressive person overall. I've actually been asking around about you after we met. I heard about the murders you solved last month. I'm guessing that's why you've been investigating Elijah's death, too?"

I opened my mouth, prepared to deny everything, but she held up a hand to stop me.

"It's okay. I know it's a weird thing to admit, but honestly, I'm happy about it. I'm glad someone cares enough to actually look into his murder. I just wish there was more I could do. I've been wracking my brain, trying to figure out who could've done this, but it's so hard to know who is guilty, and who only seems guilty. And now, with Quincy dead? You've definitely got your job cut out for you."

"I'm not sure if I'd go that far. I'm just asking some questions, but really the police are doing most of the work here. Have you thought of anything else that might be helpful? We should probably go to the police with that information."

Kristina shook her head. "Nothing that's helpful. I just can't believe he's gone. We were actually reconciling, you know? We spent the weeks leading up to his death on the phone every night, talking about our relationship and the mistakes we'd both made. I finally felt like we were getting back to how things had been before everything got complicated with the divorce."

Something clicked in my brain. Hadn't Patel told me something about the calls Elijah made before his death? Why was that relevant?

"Did you two talk about this at the college?" I asked, wracking my brain for an answer.

"No, Elijah wanted to talk over the phone. We used to do that a lot when we first started dating. We would have long phone calls because it was harder to see each other in person. We were talking on the phone in the weeks leading up to his death. He wanted to get back together and try again. I was actually the one who was a little unsure, can you believe that? If only I'd known he was going to be killed, I never would've hesitated. You can't hesitate in life, you know? You just have to go after what you want. I've been thinking about that a lot recently. It's so hard to do, but it's so important."

My body stilled as her words registered. Patel had said that Elijah had been making calls to a lawyer and to his cousin before his death, not to Kristina. Why was she claiming they were talking on the phone before he was killed?

Fortunately, Kristina was looking at something else in

the room as I slowly started to realize the truth, and she didn't seem to notice anything change in my face. She walked over to the vanity and picked up some of the things on the counter. I looked around the room as she did, trying to figure out a way out of here. Could I overpower her if I attacked her? She was wearing a sleeveless shirt today, her arm muscles bulging out. This woman had strength. No way was I overpowering her. I needed to be sneaky about this.

"I've actually been trying to get a hold of the detective on the case," I said, grabbing Kristina's attention again. "She's not answering my calls, but I know she's getting closer to the truth. If you really want to help find Elijah's killer, why don't we go down to the police station together and tell her all that we know?"

Kristina smiled and picked up something inconsequential on the vanity, looking at it from all sides. I held my breath until she put it back down.

"I don't think I'll be much help to the police," she said, turning back to me. "Like I said, I don't know very much. I think you might know the truth, though. Isn't that right? I mean, you've been asking so many people about what happened to Elijah. Don't you think it's possible you stumbled onto his killer without even realizing it?"

My head went light at her words. Was she referring to herself? Did she know what I knew? What did I even know?

"I think maybe we should go." I moved to go to the door, but Kristina was fast, and she stepped in front of the door, blocking my exit.

"I don't think that's such a good idea. I need to know what you know. What did Quincy tell you?"

My brow furrowed in confusion. "Quincy? What do you mean? He didn't tell me anything."

Kristina emitted a joyless laugh. "Oh, he knew something. He should've stayed out of things, but he figured it out. Why do you think he's dead? It has to be related."

"You think Elijah's killer went after him? But why?"

She was referring to the killer as someone else, so if I could keep her thinking that I thought that too, maybe I could get out of this.

"You're not listening. You're not seeing the truth. You're clouded by your judgment, but you need to understand, it's no one's fault. Elijah did some things he shouldn't have, but haven't we all? What's the point of any of this, if not to move on from the past?"

These were the ramblings of a guilty person. Why did I let her into my room? This wasn't going to end well.

"Kristina, I don't understand what you're saying. I think we should go, and I think you should tell the police what you know," I said, taking a step closer to her. "There are other people in this building. You're not going to get out of this in the way you think. Please, Kristina, tell me what happened."

She smirked and reached her hand into her purse. Before I understood what was going on, she whipped out a knife.

"Not so fast. I can't let you out of here. You know too much."

My gaze landed on the blade and my mouth went dry. Great, I was alone with another murderer, again.

31

My heart pounded and my vision blurred. How did I find myself face-to-face with an armed murderer again? Would Kristina stab me before I could get away? She looked pretty determined with that knife. Would anyone hear me if I screamed?

"Stop shaking." She waved the knife at me again. "You're making me nervous."

That was rich. "You're the one with the knife. Sorry if I can't keep my cool right now. I don't even understand why you're doing this. Why did you kill Elijah in the first place? Because he didn't want to get back together with you? So what? Why did that mean he had to die?"

The last time I'd faced a murderer, I'd been able to get away by keeping them talking. Maybe the same would work here.

"It wasn't just that," Kristina spat. "Elijah had been helping me with some of my bills. He said he was going to stop paying them. He said he'd decided he wanted something else for his life. If he took away that money, I wouldn't be able to keep up with the lifestyle I've become accustomed to. I told him I'd tell the college about his gambling problem if he stopped paying my bills. He said he would tell them about some other...illegal activities I partake in. He'd get fired if I talked to the college, but I'd end up in jail if he told them what I was doing. So, I apologized and said I wanted to meet up to talk about it."

"What illegal activities?"

"Not that it's any of your business, but I've been known to sample some drugs that are, let's say, frowned upon in academic circles. And in most circles, really."

I stared up at her, trying to reconcile what she was saying with the image of her I'd built up in my mind.

"It's coke, okay? Don't make a big deal out of it." She rolled her eyes.

Everything was spinning as she spoke and revealed all of this to me. How had she managed to hide all of this from everyone? A drug problem ruined lives, yet she appeared to be successful and full of life. I still had so many questions.

"Why did you meet in Pine Brook? Why that restaurant?"

Kristina scoffed, like it had been a hassle to go all the way to Pine Brook from Holliston. "I knew he'd been looking for a new apartment in this town. I figured it was best to meet somewhere where I didn't know anyone. I saw that the alley was big enough for a car, but we wouldn't be noticed if we weren't there for long. I drove my car in and we talked for a few moments, but it was clear he wasn't going to tell me anything. He didn't believe what I had to say, and he didn't want to help me. So, I got back in my car. But I was so upset. I could see him in the rearview mirror, tapping away on his phone without a care in the world. So, I put the car in reverse, and that was that."

I cringed at her casual use of the words, though I could

see the pain in her eyes. This was a woman who had made a rash decision after not getting her way, and was probably regretting it at this point. She claimed to love Elijah; was that true?

"But what about your alibi? You were on a bridge. The police never suspected you."

"Genius, right?" she said with a smirk. "I got lucky with that one. A friend asked to borrow my car that morning to see an art studio in Gig Harbor. I knew she'd have to cross over the bridge and my fast pass would get tagged. They say they take pictures when you go over the bridges, but I think they say that just to scare us into not speeding, so I figured the police wouldn't see her face. I knew my friend would keep my car in Gig Harbor long enough for me to deal with Elijah and keep suspicion off myself. I borrowed the car of another friend, and afterwards, I told her I hit a deer and would get the damage repaired out of my pocket. I didn't think I was going to get away with it, but I had to try."

"I can't believe this." She was like an evil genius. She clearly knew exactly what she was going to do when she met Elijah in that alleyway.

How did she trick all of us? She'd seemed so heartbroken at the funeral. She must've had enough time to come up with a good story and knew she could keep the police off her trail.

I needed to keep Kristina talking, and hopefully someone would interrupt us soon. Chrissy was still planning on coming to my room. Where was she?

"What about Quincy? What did he do? Why did you kill him?"

Kristina shrugged. "That really was unfortunate. Quincy was getting too close to the truth. He'd always had a thing for me. He'd try to hide it, but I could tell. When he started hanging around like a puppy dog, wanting to see me and making sure I was okay after Elijah's death, he started to notice things that he shouldn't have. Eventually, he clued into what I had done, or at least what he thought I had done. He didn't actually think I'd killed Elijah, but he thought I was keeping secrets about our relationship and our last days together. He finally confronted me and told me he knew the truth. He tried to blackmail me; can you believe that?" she asked with a shake of her head, incredulous, as if blackmail was the worst thing someone could do to another person.

I decided not to mention the fact that she was confessing to murder.

"I had no choice," she went on. "I swung at him with a pipe that was sitting out from some construction. I didn't think they'd find his body so fast, but my perfect alibi for Elijah meant the police weren't even interested in me when they found Quincy's body. I'd turned them onto that Wanda chick, and I knew your sister was looking like a good suspect, too."

"Wait, so you were the one who threatened Wanda? And who pushed me into the street? I can't believe you would do that."

She shrugged. "You were getting too close. I had no choice. Wanda was asking too many questions. I figured I could scare her off and threaten her parents. Then, with you, I saw you talking with Wanda at Elijah's office, and I knew you were getting too close to the truth. I followed you back to Pine Brook, and I saw my opportunity at that stoplight. Too bad people in this town are too likely to help each other."

A chill went through me at the thought of how close I'd gotten to death at that moment. What if Kristina had decided to stick around and finish me off? All I could think about now was getting away from her somehow.

"Well, what are you going to do now? If I start screaming, there's no way you get out of here in time." I wasn't screaming yet because the blade looked sharp, and I didn't want to get stabbed if I didn't have to.

She grabbed my arm and yanked me over to her side. "Good point about the screaming. I'm guessing you don't want to get stabbed, though. So instead, we're going to walk out of here, nice and slow. You aren't going to make any sudden movements, and I won't have to stab anyone."

She gestured with the knife for me to start walking, the tip of the blade suddenly poking into my back as I shuffled forward. I swung open the door, eager to get out of the room and into the hall where someone might see us.

Chrissy stood on the other side with her arm raised, ready to knock. An eager Estelle hung back in her shadow.

"I ran into Estelle in the lobby. We thought we could have a little meeting to figure out—" Her words halted at the sight of Kristina.

Without thinking, she rushed into the room at Kristina. I was pushed to the side, Kristina's knife flashing through the air. Pain seared through my arm as the knife slashed my skin.

"Stay back!" Kristina grabbed Chrissy's arm and pulled her close, raising the knife so that it was against her throat. "Stay back, or your sister here gets a big cut to the jugular."

My legs felt like bricks as my sister was held in place by a murderer. Fear clouded Chrissy's features as she looked wildly between Estelle and me. Kristina couldn't get away with what she was about to do.

With a yell, I threw myself at the two women, knocking us all to the ground. Chrissy screamed, curling into herself, and Kristina let out a grunt. I grabbed her arm and shook it, knocking the knife out of her hand. Estelle approached from the door and smacked Kristina in the head with her purse.

We were safe.

~

THIRTY MINUTES LATER, we stood on the front porch of the inn, watching as Kristina was led out to a squad car and put in the backseat. Another police cruiser veered into the parking lot and came to an abrupt stop. Patel slid out of the car and strode our way.

"I heard there was another attack here." She came to a stop in front of us, looking at each of us in turn. "Someone mind telling me what's going on?"

"Kristina killed Elijah and Quincy, and she came here determined to kill me, too." I stepped forward, my hands on my hips. "Chrissy and Estelle showed up, and we managed to overpower her and get her knife. That's when we called the police." I quickly explained all that Kristina had confessed to me when we were alone.

"Kristina tried to slash my throat, and Simone saved me," Chrissy said, stepping up so that she was next to me and pulling me into a side hug. I winced as she touched my arm. "Oh, sorry."

I held out my arm. Kristina's knife had sliced the skin, but we'd managed to wrap my arm in a cloth while Estelle was on the phone with the police. Would the cut from the knife scar? It might be nice to have proof of my daring escapades to show off.

Inn guests had spilled out of their rooms at the sound of all the sirens, and people from the bistro had joined the crowd in the front outside. Everyone was interested in what was going on. Just another murderer trying to wrap up loose ends at the Hemlock Inn.

"What's going to happen now?" Chrissy asked, turning to Patel. "You have to believe that I didn't kill Elijah or Quincy, right?"

"We'll need to question Kristina, to confirm what happened here and what you say happened with Elijah," Patel said. "She's already asked for an attorney, so I don't know how forthcoming she'll be, but she'll at least get brought up on charges for attacking you with a knife. I'm guessing you'll want to press charges?"

I nodded vigorously.

"I figured. Once we can find the vehicle she used to kill Elijah and find some evidence on it, we'll be able to build a case against her. We'll also make sure to confirm that someone else was driving her car over the bridge when Elijah was killed, like you said. You'll each need to give a statement and, if this case goes to trial, you may need to give evidence at the trial. But yes, it's looking like you weren't involved in any of this," Patel added to Chrissy, who squealed and wrapped the detective in a hug.

Patel stiffened, then she softened and patted Chrissy's back. She cleared her throat and stepped away from Chrissy. "My colleagues here would like to take your statements now," she said, gesturing to some officers who were approaching the inn. "We'll need to split you up and make sure your stories match. Chrissy, Estelle, you two can go with these officers."

They were led away and Patel and I watched them go.

"Thanks for coming out here so quickly," I said to Patel. "I didn't know how we were going to get out of this one. Kristina was very determined with that knife."

"Well, I'm glad we got this figured out. You did a good job here, even though you shouldn't put others at risk or confront a suspected killer without telling me what you're doing."

"I tried calling you! Learn to keep your phone off silent. Detective," I added with a smile to soften my words. "I don't know how I would've gotten out of that if Chrissy and Estelle hadn't come by."

Patel smiled. "You surround yourself with some pretty interesting people. Just try to stay out of any future murder investigations."

I nodded, though even I knew that wasn't a promise I could keep. These cases kept coming to me; how could I stay away?

32

The next day, I came downstairs to the lobby of the inn, reeling from the events of the previous day.

"Good morning, detective," Tracy said from the front desk when I came down. "I heard you had another exciting night. It's all anyone can talk about."

My cheeks warmed at the thought of people talking about me uncovering another murderer. The police probably wouldn't be happy to hear that people were referring to me as a detective.

"I really should stop getting involved in these things. At some point, it can't be good for business."

Tracy shrugged. "We've actually had a rush of new bookings this morning. It seems like murder is exactly what this old inn needs to stay in business. Besides, you're just doing what you think is right. Though I wouldn't recommend meeting up alone with killers anymore. I'd prefer it if my business partner didn't get herself murdered."

"I think I can do that," I said with a smile.

A large platter with a sticker on the side sat in front of Tracy at the desk. Taking a closer look, I read "Pine Brook

Antiques" on the sticker, plus a dollar amount that caused my eyebrows to shoot up my head.

"What's this?" I asked Tracy, motioning to the platter.

Her grin was wide, her nose ring sparkling in her face. "Isn't it wonderful? I finally found something that the antiques people said had real value! They quoted me that price and everything."

Wow. With this price, we could get the leak in the back ceiling fixed, order Hank new pots and pans, and make sure we always had enough wood for the fireplace. Tracy's recent obsession with antiques might finally pay off.

"Wow, this is amazing. Where do we sell it?"

Tracy looked at me in confusion. "Sell it? We're not going to sell it. It's an original Wellington!" she said as if I should know the name. "This baby is going to bring in so many more guests than selling it could ever hope to do. We've already had three new reservations ever since the antiques fair announced we have the platter. I just need to find someplace to display it."

My heart sank at her words, though it seemed only right. How silly of me to think that this antique should be sold, rather than displayed for all to stare at? I pushed out thoughts of a new stove for the kitchen and focused back on the front desk.

A few minutes later, Chrissy came down the stairs with her duffel bag slung over her shoulder. I hurried to her side and helped her get it down the stairs.

"What's this?" I asked, looking between her and the bag. "Are you leaving?"

I'd been hoping we could have a couple days of normal sister time, without a murder hanging over our heads, but it looked like that wasn't going to be the case. She had things to deal with at home, and it was probably best that she left to deal with them.

Chrissy nodded. "I think it's time for me to go home. I talked to that detective, and she said I didn't need to stay in town. I called Mark last night and told him everything. I just want to see him and Hannah again. It's time I face up to what I left and actually try to handle my marriage. I shouldn't have run away from my problems. After what happened yesterday, I don't want to go another day without dealing with the people I love. Thank you for letting me stay here while I figured all of this out. And thanks for, you know, saving my life." Her smile was wide.

I pulled her into a hug, my chest filling with positive vibes. "I'm so proud of you. You know you're always welcome here, but I agree that it's best to go home and handle things there. And maybe the next time you visit, we won't find a dead body."

I could only hope that was true, but given how things were turning out, was this going to be my last body?

"I'll keep my fingers crossed," Chrissy said with a laugh. "You know, it's interesting. I've spent so much time interested in true crime and reading about all these wild things that happen in the world. Now that I've seen my first dead body, I really hope it's my last. It's much spookier when it happens to you." She shivered as she remembered the events of the past few days.

It didn't help that we'd been threatened by a murderer the day before. It wasn't an easy thing to go through, and it was going to take us both some time before we felt safe again. But at least we had each other.

"Please be safe up here. No more confronting killers on your own. I still want to have a sister after all of this."

Chrissy pulled me into a tight hug, then went outside to her rental car.

She was right, and I would try to be careful. I waved after her and watched her go, pleased that we'd at least gotten some time to bond before she left. I was also hopeful that I wouldn't run into any more killers anytime soon.

I'd spoken with Patel late last night. Kristina had started confessing as soon as they got her into the squad car, and Patel wanted to keep me updated. I'd made sure to ask her about Marcus. I'd been so convinced about his guilt, so I'd needed to know why he'd been acting so weird.

"Kristina owned up to that," Patel had said. "Apparently, she knew Marcus was in town and knew about his history with Elijah and Quincy. She figured if she could keep him in town, she could get the police to look at him as a suspect. She told him she had his money and would give it to him if he waited a few days, but she was dragging it out. I think she was hoping we would find more incriminating evidence against him and arrest him."

I'd been so convinced that Marcus was the killer, and Kristina had told me so many things about him that made him seem guilty. Was I almost tricked into helping an innocent man get arrested for a crime he didn't commit?

"You were right about Kristina and Elijah not reconciling," Patel had gone on. "We finally heard back from that lawyer Elijah had been calling before his death. Apparently, he'd been paying for some of Kristina's things even after their divorce, and he was trying to figure out how he could untangle himself from her completely. I guess he wanted out of their entire relationship."

That explained the phone calls and confirmed that Kristina had been lying about their reconciliation. She'd had everyone fooled with this sad widow act, when really Elijah had been trying to get away from her.

Patel also confirmed how Kristina had fabricated her alibi.

"Those bridges do take photos of the cars passing through, but you have to specifically request that in your warrant," she'd explained. "At first, we only got a warrant to see the license plates tagged. Once we realized Kristina was lying, we were able to pull the right records and now have an image of someone else driving Kristina's car into Gig Harbor. We're still looking for the friend that was actually driving to confirm she was there, but it's clear in the photo that it's not Kristina."

It was a genius alibi, and I would have been more impressed if Kristina weren't a killer. Still, I was glad to know Elijah's murderer was finally in jail.

Back at the inn, Tracy turned to me with a grin. "By the way, these showed up for you." She waved a set of keys in the air. I'd been so focused on thinking about the murders, it took me a moment to realize what she was holding.

"I got the place?" A smile bloomed across my face at the realization of what this meant.

"You got the place." Tracy grinned and tossed me the keys.

Now I could finally feel like I was living in my own space and truly settling in Pine Brook. We'd be able to make some serious money by booking the onsite suite, and Tracy and I would keep running this place like true partners.

"Now I just need to find some furniture to fill up the place," I said, twirling the keys around my finger. "Any suggestions?"

"I think I might be able to help out," a male voice

answered. Nick had entered the lobby and walked over to the front desk.

My stomach did a flip at the sight of him. "Oh really? Know of any good places?"

"I do. I actually know a few people with good deals nearby. I'm sure we can find you some pretty great furniture to fill up the space. I'm glad you decided to take the apartment," he added, leaning his arms against the countertop.

"Well, it's a good unit. Remind me where you live?" Maybe we wouldn't see each other as much as I thought we might.

"Right above you," Nick said with a smile. "I guess we'll be seeing a lot more of each other."

"I guess so." It wasn't so bad to live so close to Nick, was it? He was a good friend and, who knows? Maybe that friendship could turn into something more.

"Why don't we go check out your new place now?" Nick asked, slipping the keys out of my hands and tossing them into the air once, a smirk on his face. "You should make sure you still like it."

Tracy was watching us, her eyes twinkling and her lips pressed together like she was holding in a laugh.

"I'm all good here. You should go check out your new place," she said with a wink. I bet that wasn't the only thing she thought I should check out.

I turned back to Nick, heat spreading across my face to match my grin. "Let's go."

I followed him out into the morning sun, taking a deep breath of fresh air. I was overthinking everything. What's the worst that could happen?

THANKS FOR READING!

If you enjoyed reading about Simone and the Hemlock Inn, I'd love it if you could leave a review on Amazon and Goodreads. Honest reviews of my books help bring them to the attention of other readers.

Medicine and Murder, Book 3 in the Hemlock Inn Mysteries series, is available now! Head to Amazon.com to pick up a copy today!

ACKNOWLEDGMENTS

I'm so grateful for the opportunity to write these books and share them with the world, and so many others helped me along the way to get this book in your hands.

Thanks to Max, as always, for supporting my dreams and brainstorming causes of death to keep these books interesting. Thanks to my beta readers, Ashley and Dimitra, for your fabulous feedback when this story was in a much rougher form. Thanks to my editor, Carmen, for helping me discover more about these characters and bringing their personalities to the page.

And thanks to you, dear reader, for picking up another one of my books and making it to the end. I hope it was a fun ride!

ABOUT THE AUTHOR

Josephine Smith is an author of cozy mysteries. A Washington state native, Josephine now makes her home in Northern California with her husband and dog and cat. She loves all things sweet, foods and people included, and can be found with her nose buried in a book. Visit her website at www.josephinesmithauthor.com, or connect on social media at Josephine Smith, Author (Facebook and Instagram).

Come say hello!